# Sex & Other Acts
# of the Imagination
## *(Stories)*
### Cliff Burns

Cover design: Chris Kent

Cover art: "Figure" by Cliff Burns

Interior layout & design: Daniel Middleton | Scribe Freelance


Published by Black Dog Press (blackdogpress@yahoo.ca)

Printed by Lightning Source


ISBN: 978-0-9938721-0-5

*for Sherron, who was there right from the beginning*

# Acknowledgements

"Apocalypse Beach" appeared in *Chimera Connections* and *Portents*

"Invisible Boy" appeared in *Midnight Graffiti*, *Tesseracts 3* & on "Ambience" (CBC Radio)

"Walt Disney in Hell" appeared in *Chimera Connections*

"Carl" appeared in *New Blood*

"The Cattletruck" appeared in *Midnight Graffiti* (Warner Books) and *The Village Idiot*

"The Strange Music" appeared in *Verve*

"Snow Angels" appeared in *Thin Ice #3*

"Sex*Tet: A Horrific Medley of Old Favorites" was xcerpted in *Ransom*, *Grue* and *New Blood*

"Teenage Wasteland" appeared in *Ouroboros*

"Public Enemy" appeared in *Not One Of Us*

"Dry" appeared in *Western People Magazine*

"Old Friends" appeared in *Vice Versa*

"Live! From Planet Earth!" appeared in *Starsong*

"Man Disassembling" appeared in *EOTU* and *The Best of EOTU '89*

"Arrival" appeared in *Revelations from Yuggoth* and *Chronoscope*

"Final Showing" appeared in *Bone-Chilling Tales* and *The Haunted Journal*

"Monologue" appeared in *Deep South Journal*

"The Hibakusha" appeared in *Iniquities*, *Noctulpa* and on "Ambience" (CBC Radio)

# Contents

# Introduction
## by Cliff Burns

Twenty-five years is a long time, at least from a human perspective. I'm a very different person today than I was back in 1990. Less angry, more passionate. Wiser and deeper, the passage of time and hard won experience adding layers, a whole other dimension to my character, while exacting a toll on me physically and spiritually.

Obviously I'm a better writer than I was a quarter century ago, my aesthetic more mature and refined, my "style" more sophisticated. But, again, what I've gained quality-wise must be weighed against something that's been lost.

The stories in this collection are unquestionably cruder, less "literary" than my recent work, but they are also looser, brasher, more emotional and raw, refreshingly devoid of self-consciousness...and maybe some of that's missing from my newer fiction (to its detriment). Those are the first thoughts that come to mind as I page through my very first book. I'm also struck my how dark *Sex & Other Acts of the Imagination* is, how (yes) mean-spirited at times.

I find myself taken aback by how many of the central or pivotal players are so passive—either compliant victims or cowardly on-lookers. Contrast that with a character like Evgeny Nightstalk (from my novel *So Dark the Night*), the ultimate man of action. Talk about a sea change.

All things considered, I still find much to like in this collection. It contains my first "breakthrough" effort, "Invisible Boy", a tale that nabbed a few choice anthology appearances, as well as undimmed gems like "Walt Disney in Hell (A Trilogy)", "The Cattletruck" and, a personal favorite, "The Strange Music".

Sadly, I must report that a story that appeared in the 1990 edition of *Sex* has been dropped this time around due to copyright concerns. "The Murder of John Lennon: A Collage" incorporated snippets from various Beatles and John Lennon songs, a sentence from *Catcher in the Rye,* and I could foresee all kinds of legal complications that might ensue if I retained the tale. Life is too short to take on corporate vultures representing the likes of Sony and the Michael Jackson estate. No thanks.

That decision depressed me until I remembered another tale, "Snow Angels", that had just missed sneaking on to the roster back in 1990. I had to go digging in my archives but I found a small press 'zine it appeared in, gave it a quick polish and hereby present this previously uncollected story for your entertainment and edification.

I'm delighted to be re-issuing *Sex & Other Acts of the Imagination*—its release marked a pivotal moment in my creative life; it represents a leap of faith and a remarkable act of self-empowerment. It was my first venture into self-publishing and, who knows, if it had bombed I might not be where or *who* I am today. Happily, it did very well, exceeding expectations by selling out its print run in less than five months. Copies of that first edition are very dear these days, fetching a king's ransom (another reason I decided to bring the book back into print).

I want to emphasize that I came to self-publishing as a last resort. My *Sex* collection was turned down by every significant press in North America (and a number in Great Britain too). To a man/woman their representatives assured me that short story collections don't sell, especially short story collections by young, Canadian authors. It didn't help that the majority of my tales fell into the "horror" or "dark fantasy" category—speculative fiction has always been a bugbear to most agents and editors, many refusing to touch the stuff with a long, pointy-ended stick.

Around that time (late 1980s), my girlfriend, Sherron (now my wife of many years), made a trip to Toronto and encountered a guy, kind of a creepy- looking character, selling copies of his chapbooks on a street corner. That eccentric entrepreneur was none other than the legendary Crad Kilodney, literary bad boy, scourge of CanLit and other hidebound Canadian institutions. Sherron bought a copy of a booklet Crad wrote called *Bang Heads Here Suffering Bastards* and gave it to me as a gift. That thoughtful act turned out to be integral in my decision to publish the *Sex* collection myself. If Crad could do it...

But I have to say, my decision to go the independent (indie) route probably had more to do with my psychology and personal character. There's a streak of ornery contrariness that runs through me like a high voltage wire. Since childhood I have been unwilling to allow anyone control over my life. I have an innate distrust of people, especially authority figures, a complicated psychology that adamantly insists that I must, at all times, have complete autonomy over my own affairs. Beholden to none. A master of my own fate.

I think that's one reason why I so ruthlessly protect the integrity of my work—it is an extension of me, of the ideas and themes and preoccupations that help define who I am. Those who attempt to tamper with or dilute or "shape" my writing soon learn, to their great chagrin, the lengths I'll go to to deter and frustrate them. Some of my encounters with editors, agents, film folk and entertainment lawyers (recounted on my blog, *Beautiful Desolation*) are the stuff of legend. On occasion they've led to real ugliness. Expletives, threats of physical violence, numerous times when I've read people the riot act. I can be a real fucking pitbull when I'm provoked. No exaggeration.

Y'see, it's that power thing again. Agents, editors, movie producers, etc. automatically assume mere authors should defer to them, fawn over them for a few scraps of praise and a scatter of silver.

*Bullshit*, I say.

Anyone who works with me has to accept that *my* aesthetic, *my* vision is paramount. No other input is required. I am not seeking collaborators or creative partners. It is that highly individualistic and personal approach to writing that makes my body of work so unique and distinctive. I will allow *no one* to usurp my position as primary creator or exploit what Rimbaud calls "the sacred disorder of my mind".

Arrogant? Pompous? Elitist? Yes, I've had those words frequently lobbed in my direction and, really, my only line of defense is pointing at my novels and stories and saying *see for yourself.*

Because in the final analysis it's the *work* that distinguishes the genius from the dolt, the inspired from the derivative. My fiction either measures up or it doesn't...and it only takes a few paragraphs to discern if a scribbler has "the right stuff". But the playing field is getting awfully crowded and it's harder and harder to find readers when they have so many books and e-books and what have you to choose from.

The last twenty-five years have seen colossal changes in the publishing business and for devotees of the printed word the news isn't encouraging. Since the multi-nationals took over the major publishing houses, the quality of writing has sunk to new lows. What few intelligent, literate, astute editors and agents there were under the old regime found themselves forced out by their corporate masters or quit the scene in despair. The new breed are little more than drones, fixated on the bottom line, earning their performance bonus, finding the latest bestseller, which is usually only a slight variation on the last Big Book.

Maxwell Perkins? Isn't that a brand of coffee?

I haven't read a popular title in ages and avoid the "New Release" section of bookstores like a rabid, incontinent skunk. I have to look further and further afield for good writing, quality books and, increasingly, I'm finding them with small or "alternative" publishers, university imprints, independent presses. If literature hopes to survive, these are the people who will carry that flickering torch, preserving it against the agents of stupidity, homogeneity and mediocrity.

The indie approach allowed me to permanently bypass

the gate-keepers of traditional publishing and for that I shall always be grateful. It granted me direct access to readers around the world; one positive change over the past two (+) decades is the growing prominence of the internet. Talk about a networking tool! Twenty-five years ago we didn't have blogging, Facebook, print on demand publishing, etc. Hard to believe.

These days, authors have a plethora of publishing platforms to choose from, all sorts of media and devices we can employ to promote and distribute our work. And that's great.

But it's also led to that aforementioned *deluge* of self-published titles by folks with little or no understanding of vocabulary, grammar, syntax. Sub-literate twits aping their favorite authors or TV shows, twenty-first century fan fiction, possessing all the skill and artistry of a velvet oil painting of the Last Supper. These books should never have been *written*, let alone issued an ISBN prefix and dumped on Amazon. Amateurs and wannabes taking a whack at fame and fortune. Easy money. I wish they'd buy a lottery ticket instead, saving vast stands of timber from needless massacre.

As an independent author and "self-publisher", I feel there is an onus on me to somehow counteract or nullify this plague of amateurism by releasing the most technically proficient, well-executed books I possibly can. I seek smart, discerning readers but I also recognize the need to reward those good souls with exciting, daring ideas and images, literature that makes its impact felt even in a world moving at breakneck speed, a hundred different distractions tempting and enticing us every single waking moment of our lives. And that's why it is so *essential* that I maintain the highest literary and aesthetic standards, refusing to cater to the marketplace or concede to bland expectations.

For the past thirty years I have expended every ounce of my creative energy stimulating, surprising and provoking my readership, however small or scattered it might be. I don't see that approach changing any time soon.

The *stories* keep me honest. Refusing to be ignored, a constant clamor in my mind, a dozen different voices demanding a chance to be heard. Issuing from the depths of some etheric realm or collective unconscious, addressing universal human themes, reflecting our frailties *and* our enormous promise as a species.

One day, with our God-given imagination, we might inherit the stars.

Unless, of course, our inner demons prevent us.

You know the ones I'm talking about. Their faces immediately familiar, their names older than sin.

*August, 2014*

## Apocalypse Beach

It's sunset.

You're sitting on the beach, sitting on the cool, white sand with your arms wrapped around your legs and your head is back and you're listening to the breakers and you're dying.

Part of you wishes that the cataracts clouding your vision would miraculously dissolve away, affording you one last look at the world, one last viewing of the sun drowning in the limitless sea. But then you remember the bodies; you can smell them, you know they're there, roiling in the surf, sprawled along the shoreline like soldiers cut down in some beach-head assault. Maybe it's better this way.

*BOOM        BOOM        BOOM*

Memory has claimed all the sights and sounds you once associated with this beach, the squawking birds, the blaring radios, the jocks, the kids, the bikinis, all gone, now there is only

*BOOM*        *BOOM*        *BOOM*

And.

The smell. The smell is very bad. But you stay. You stay because.

The breeze is nice...as long as you don't breathe it. Just let it play across you like a light, flickering tongue, tousling your hair, sharpening your nipples, caressing your genitals. But don't *breathe* it. Because if you breathe it you'll know. That it's necrophilia. You're making it with a dead thing.

The sun is almost gone. The sun is waving good-bye. The sun is collecting its toys and going home. It doesn't want to play with you anymore.

But the breeze stays on. It plays doctor with your sightless, scabby, grotesque body and you let it. You let it because it's the only friend you have left.

The tide is coming in. The tide will soon tug at you insistently, wanting to add another dash of humanity to the Pacific Stew.

All your life you have feared death. Death was proof that God was unkind and perhaps even evil. Now you see it differently.

Death no longer exists in caricature, a mocking, strutting nothingness brandishing a set of immutable chains and raking your nightmares with ghastly laughter. Now death has stepped into the open and you see it for what it is. You admire its lean-ness, its logic, its unfaltering devotion to its mission.

And although you don't have a religious experience *per se* and no master plan is revealed to you, during your final moments you do find a kind of peace.

As the darkness settles over you, you don't fight it, you don't writhe, you don't kick and scream. You lie back on the cool sand. And you wait. Inside your head. You wait. For that stinging kiss.

## Invisible Boy

I hate it when she ties into me in front of the kid. He just stands there all bug-eyed while she reams me out.

"I won't—WILL NOT—have you smoking that shit in *my* house, in front of *my* son. Are you listening to me? Do...you...understand? You're not only screwing up your life and my life—what about his? There are other people around here, y'know. What's he supposed to think?" She points at Jeff but he just hangs his head.

"What's the big deal, Sal? It's only a joint for Chrissakes. What about all the times he's seen you so drunk you don't recognize him? I don't hear you talking about that."

"Don't you dare—" she starts to say.

"I'm just telling it like it us," I fire back.

"—insult me in front of my son. Don't you dare do that again, Ray. You'll be making the biggest mistake of your life."

She puts her hand on Jeff's head; he looks really surprised that she's actually touching him.

"Oh, I see. Now he's *your* son. What about all those long windy speeches about how we're one big, happy family?"

"Ted would never have—"

And then I really blow my stack. "Ted, Ted, Ted. That fucker practically permeates this place. You still got pictures of him hanging up, you still call him at least once a month, rain or shine. But, hell, that's all right with me. I love helping Ma Bell out with a few marathon long distance phone calls. Jesus *Christ*, Sally, you've been separated for five years... and divorced for three. When are you gonna cut the cord? The guy's a *jerk*." I see Jeff flinch when I say it but it's said so I keep right on plugging. "He doesn't want to help support Jeff, doesn't even want any pictures of him, never sends any money at Christmas and here I am busting my hump to keep the fridge filled week in and week out and not getting any credit—"

"Jeff, go to your room," Sally says, cold as ice.

"He tried going to his room!" I bellow and Jeff twitches again. "But you decided to use him as a prop in this little show you're putting on."

She gives me THE LOOK. Yup, I'll be sleeping on the couch again tonight. Shouldn't have let the dope do the talking.

God, I feel bad for that kid. I go out of my way to avoid scraps with Sally but she just keeps picking at me and picking at me like I'm an itchy scab. And every time we fight she manages to get a few good ones in under the belt. Like that crack about Ted.

The dope was nothing. Hey, we've shared a joint lots of nights after Jeff's gone to bed. She really likes the stuff. Except every time she gets high she gets these wild cravings and we have to order out for pizza or Chinese food.

I got home from work and neither her or Jeff was around so I decided to roll myself a little number to help me unwind. I was finishing it off, listening to some BTO on the radio (cranked wayyyyy up) when her and Jeff walked in.

WHAM!

She'd had a rough day too and seeing me standing there with a roach burning between my fingers was enough to set her off. You should never sneeze in avalanche country, right?

On the way to his bedroom Jeff digs some comic books out of one of the shopping bags they carried in. As he shuffles down the hall his nose is already buried in the latest issue of *Spiderman*. Poor little bugger. Spidey's probably his best friend in the world. I'd like to go in and sit on the end of his bed, talk to him, maybe read through his comics with him—some of them are pretty good, y'know—but Sally starts yipping at me and I yap back and by the time we wear ourselves out it's after nine.

As soon as there's a break in the action I go and look in on Jeff. He's got all of his sheets and blankets wadded up in the middle of his bed. He's under that pile somewhere; I can hear him singing away, maybe plugged into his Walkman. I tell him good night but I don't think he hears me. I turn out the light and leave him to his soundproof sanctuary.

Jeez, I wonder if Sal's seen this latest trick. I mean, I'm thinking this can't be a good sign. The kid is pulling back from us, maybe developing some kind of, you know, problem because of—of what goes on around here. That isn't right. What we're doing to that boy isn't right.

I wish I could spend more time with him. I work during

the week and on weekends it's Sally I have to pay attention to or I'm in one deep pile of doo-doo as my good friend George Bush would say. Now and then we're alone together. I'll take him along when I go to the store or I'll swing by and pick him up after school. He barely says a word the whole time we're together. Mostly just "yes" and "no" or just shrugging. I wonder what he thinks about me living at the house, sleeping in the same bed as her. Even at his age kids know that grown-ups aren't playing checkers in there.

I keep buying him presents. I know it looks bad, like I'm trying to buy his love but I can't help myself. So every once in awhile we have to act out this ritual: I push a model or some space toy across the table to him and try to decipher his mumbles as he picks it up and looks it over. I know he likes my presents, I see him playing with them all the time. I think he's afraid to show too much enthusiasm because then she'll have something to use against him. She's constantly threatening to take his toys away if he's not good. And the thing is HE IS GOOD. Too damn good. He's like a well-trained pet. He fetches when she wants him to and speaks when she wants him to but most of the time it's like she just wants him to play dead.

When I come back into the kitchen everything's pretty well back to normal. Whatever that means. I ask Sally what the plans are for the weekend and get a funny look.

"Same as always," she says. Like it's final.

Every weekend it's the same thing. We buy groceries, pick up some booze and a couple of videos and stay cooped up like parakeets until Monday. I've tried to get her to go to the beach or the park at least. I tell her we can roast some wienies, drink some beer, chuck the Frisbee around, have ourselves a great time. Y'know, like a real family. She doesn't want the hassle of packing a lunch and hates the long, hot drive and dirty, smelly bathrooms and the bugs and the people and the loud music...so we end up sitting on our butts doing nothing.

I wonder if she'd let Jeff and me go off by ourselves next year, maybe take a week and go camping. I know she hates the idea of being alone. The woman is incapable of entertaining herself. She says that's what men are for. One of these days when I'm good and drunk I'm gonna ask her: wassa matter? Did Ted run out of jokes?

She'll cut me off for a whole fucking year for it but it'll be worth it. Every time she brings that guy up it just galls me. Her first love. Her high school sweetheart. The man she gave her virginity to. What a crock. I think he's done more damage to Jeff than anybody. How would I have felt if my old man had turned his back on me? Like I was worthless. And I'm sure that's exactly how he feels.

Saturday morning Jeff and I are watching "Tom and Jerry" cartoons and yukking it up and she comes storming in and starts yelling at him 'cause his room's a mess. I mean, what kid's isn't, right? But she totally shits on him, calls him lazy and stupid and irresponsible. He's cowering on the floor like a sick puppy. Me, stupid ass that I am, I just sit there like a bump on a log and say nothing. He shuts the t.v. off and goes meekly to his room. Sally sits at the table drinking coffee and smoking, glaring at me, daring me to say something. I wait until she goes to take her shower then I go in to lend Jeff a hand—but he's already got everything cleaned up and gone outside.

I can hear Sally singing in the bathroom; she sounds as happy as a lark. As I walk past she comes out and gives me a big kiss and makes her way singing and dancing to the kitchen to start breakfast. When it's ready I call out the back door to Jeff—

And here he comes, walking out of his bedroom like some kind of zombie and sitting down at the table. His face looks puffy and he's pale and all sweaty. I want to say something about him playing hide-and-seek on me but he's acting so weird that I skip that and instead lean over and ask him if he's feeling okay—and he nearly jumps out of his skin.

"Uncle Ray asked you a question, Jeff," Sally prods him.

"Everything all right?" I'm smiling at him, trying to keep it nice and friendly but I can see his bottom lip trembling and I *know* that if I keep pushing he's going to start blubbering. So I change the subject, start telling Sally about something that happened at work. But I keep an eye on him all through breakfast. Something is definitely bugging him. I can tell he's not hungry but he's forcing himself to eat because if he doesn't she'll get p.o.'d and not let him have any dinner or supper. He chews carefully because she hates noisy eaters.

When he's finished he wipes his mouth with a napkin, pushes his chair back , puts his plate in the sink. Then he asks to be excused, slips on his jacket and shoes and goes outside. Don't ask me what he does.

"What do you think about going to see a movie tonight?" I ask, really neutral.

"Is there anything good in town?" Already she's frowning. Sensing that her monotonous routine is about to be disrupted.

"Yeah, 'Dumbo' is playing at the Coronet. Man, I loved that show when I was a kid."

"Don't be stupid," she snaps. "I don't want to see that crap."

"I thought Jeff would really get a kick out of—"

"It's another stupid cartoon!" She's getting steamed and there's nothing I can do about it. "That's all he ever watches. When is he supposed to get a dose of reality?"

"I think the trouble is that he gets too much reality for his own good—especially around here." I could bite my tongue off as I say it.

"YOU GO TO HELL!" She yells and tramps off to the bedroom and makes a lot of noise.

That night there are no movies, not even on video. When

Jeff asks about watching t.v. he's sent to his room without any supper. When I try to veto that she looks at me all calm and cool and tells me to go fuck myself.

Jeff trudges off. As he passes me on the way to his room I try to catch his eye. But it's like he's looking right through me. I can see that he's scared, man, more scared than a kid has a right to be.

That's when I start thinking about getting out, just saying "screw this" and taking off. It's so tempting. Escape from this crazy woman, take up with my riff-raff friends again, get drunk, get stoned, do anything I want—

—and then I remember the times when she's soft, when she fixes herself up and talks sensibly and laughs and gives me sexy looks. I love that person more than anything. More than I love myself. And there's Jeff. Some part of me deep and secret connects with that boy. I think we'll be close some day, him and me. I'm almost positive about that.

I stay.

I must be crazy but I always end up staying.

Later on, I go to the john and when I finish up in there I wander a little further down the hall, knock on Jeff's door, stick my head inside.

The room is empty.

And this time I make sure: I check the closet and even take a quick peek under the bed.

I'm about to close the door, I'm wondering where he could have gone—and I hear this little sigh. I lean into the room again but there's no one there. So, okay, I *didn't* hear a little sigh.

I close the door and start back down the hallway—

The bedroom door opens behind me.

And I just *freeze*, like, in mid-step. Turn around really slow. The doorway is empty. Very weird. I approach timidly, reach out to shut it and that's when I hear a voice, a voice as small as a mouse, coming from somewhere in the room.

"…please…Uncle Ray…please…"

"Jeff?" I edge inside, trying to locate him.

"…help me, please…I can't make it back!"

My foot bumps into a small leg that isn't there. As I kneel a boy-sized hand slips inside mine, gripping my fingers tightly.

"Please," he whimpers, "I—I'm scared, Uncle Ray.

Please...please help me..."

"Okay," I promise and the invisible boy comes to me and I hold him close.

## Walt Disney in Hell
### (A Trilogy)

*"I'll see you in Disneyland."*

*—Richard Ramirez ("The Night Stalker", serial killer)*
*to spectators as he is led away after receiving the death*
*sentence*

### I

Walt Disney is building amusement parks in Hell. Rollercoasters cascade into loop-de-loops lined with glistening razor blades that eviscerate the riders. Patrons wait patiently to enter haunted houses boasting real ghouls, flesh eaters and blood suckers and vivisectionists that giggle and caper through the corridors, slicing and dicing with insane abandon. Ferris wheels constructed without the benefit of safety bars upend suddenly, flinging screaming people to the ground. Conscientious employees sweep up the mess, hose down the rides, prepare for the next horde of sinners.

## II

Walt Disney has taken a male lover, a young boy who hung himself with shoelaces while awaiting trial for killing his parents with an ax. The kid gives great head. Walt likes it when he goes down on him while he's working at his desk, poring over blueprints for sadistic new rides. After Walt comes the kid has to put on a set of mouse ears and in falsetto squeaks tell Walt what a wonderful, big cock he has.

## III

Walt Disney and P.T. Barnum talk shop while drinking a concoction known as "Old Nick". Walt thinks the Devil thinks too small and Barnum agrees. They bicker on conditions for the merger, finally conclude negotiations with a handshake. The Devil will be deposed and a massive amusement park built that encompasses all of the regions of Hell. It will take eons to accomplish but, as Walt looks at it, when he was living he started out with a skinny fucking mouse and a dream and forged an empire. Why shouldn't history repeat itself?

# Carl

When he was a baby, Carl was long and thin and pale. This is a picture of him in his sailor outfit. Doesn't he look cute? And look at his eyes. In one of her songs—I forget which one—Joan Baez sings about "eyes bluer than robin's eggs". Carl's eyes were like that.

Here's one taken when he was four. He looks like a little bird. But isn't he beautiful? And those eyes. The way he looks at the camera, like he's got a deep, dark secret.

That's him with his Uncle Fred. You know *that* story, don't you? Oh, that's a juicy one, let me tell you.

Fred just loved Carl. He'd go over and visit him as often as he could and whenever he went he'd take him a present. He was always grabbing at Carl and holding him and cuddling up to him. No one realized that him and the boy had this sick thing going and all that hugging and squeezing was part of it.

It was Carl's mother who found him out. She walked in and caught him at—at what he was doing and started screaming and cursing and old Fred was lucky to get out of there alive. He wasn't ever allowed back in the house. And whenever he sent Carl something for his birthday or Christmas it got sent right back. You never heard about any of this? And here I thought everyone knew.

Here's Carl again...he's ten here, I think. Yes, he was ten that summer. He still doesn't have very much meat on his bones. He's getting taller though. I think he looks really...really dignified. He loved sports but, you know, he wasn't very good at them. I remember once he broke his nose playing baseball. Went to catch a fly ball and got it right splat in the face. This was taken when he was...um...I think he's thirteen here. Maybe twelve. *That* was the year he got molested by that teacher. Roberts. Paul Roberts was his name.

The marks should have given it away. Carl's marks that year were awful. And he was such a good student, no *As* but he always came pretty close. This Roberts guy was his home room teacher and he'd make excuses to get Carl alone with him and—well, I don't think I need to go into the gory details. I think you know what I mean. Because his marks were dropping, he had to make an appointment with the school counselor. It took awhile but she finally got him to blurt it all out. The teacher was suspended, there was talk of a trial but nothing ever came of it. Knowing the way this world works he's probably teaching somewhere else, committing his perversions on other children.

This is Carl's fifteenth birthday. That's his one good pal, Doug Lucyshyn. He didn't invite anyone else so his mother called over some of her friends so they could make it a party. That's Carol Drieson, a woman who worked with his mother. She's another skeleton rattling around in the family closet. You mean you don't know about that either?

Well, what happened was that a couple of days after the party Carol asked Carl if he'd come over and clean out her garage. She offered him twenty-five dollars and right away he said yes because, like most teenagers, he was broke all the time. Now I don't know the full story but what I understand is that after Carl was finished in the garage he went into the house to collect the money and...um...Carol and him...to me it's perfectly obvious that she seduced him. They ended up in the bedroom and...all that. I imagine Carl was scared to death but she wasn't going to take no for an answer and anyway he didn't know any better. All of this is just between you, me and the walls, okay? Just some innocent gossip, right?

I gather Carl was pretty upset by what happened. He was always really quiet but for quite awhile afterward he hardly said a word to anyone. Even Doug couldn't get much out of him.

This one Carl gave me. That's him and Lisa. I liked her a lot. I guess that's why he gave it to me. Cute, eh? They look a lot alike when they're standing side by side like that, don't you think? And they were alike in many ways. They were both shy and got embarrassed easily and had the same sly sense of humor. They would say something and it would take you all day before you figured out they were trying to be funny. I was as surprised as everyone else when they broke up. I have my suspicions about that. I think she had it pretty rough at home. That's just a feeling but I've learned to trust my feelings. She was always acting really spooked and if you raised your voice, even if you were laughing, she'd kind of shrink back. Carl didn't make her that way. Something to do with her family, I'm sure of it.

After Lisa there was Denise. I think she's...flip to the next page...that's her there. Denise was Lisa's best friend. You couldn't imagine two people more different. Denise was really out-going, really...well, not loud but—boisterous, that's a good word. It was hard to get a word in edgewise with that girl. She'd do all the talking and Carl would sit there like a statue. Oh, she was all right I guess but I was glad to hear he wasn't seeing her any more. One thing used to drive me crazy. She used to grab his hand and hold it between both of hers, hold onto it *tight* like she was afraid he was going to take off on her. I don't know. I thought it looked kind of pathetic.

After Denise and him split up Carl didn't have much more to do with girls. He concentrated on his schoolwork and his grades showed steady improvement. In Grade Twelve his marks were third highest in his class. Got a copy of his transcript at the back of the album. Have a look.

After he graduated he decided to take a crack at university. We were all really proud of him for that. None of us had been smart enough to go.

Carl didn't do very well at university. The way he explained it to me once was that the atmosphere was different. The professors didn't care if you showed up late for classes or if you showed up at all. They were getting paid to teach, not babysit. The one thing Carl couldn't get over was the way they swore in front of their students. They'd be right in the middle of a lesson and they'd say "shit" or "goddamn" or "bastard" or something worse. Let me ask you, is that teaching? He lasted about a semester and a half and then he dropped out. No one got down on him about it or made him feel like he'd failed or anything—until he went and got that job at the restaurant. That upset his folks a lot.

I mean, here's this kid, this smart kid, he's got twelve years of schooling plus some university classes and he's washing bloody dishes! You can see why we might be a little disappointed in him. We all had such big plans for Carl. Even I got on his case once and asked him what the story was. He told me he really liked working in the restaurant. For the first time in his life he could relax, put his mind on hold. See, the dishwasher was stuck away from everyone else so most of the time he didn't have to talk to people or get along with anybody.

I remember the first time he mentioned his manager, that Nona woman. I don't want to say anything bad about her but it was clear right from the start that she gave Carl the willies. It's all come out, you know, about how she used to harass the young boys working there, pinching them on the bum and talking dirty to them. I think the woman was a bit of a cuckoo bird myself. She was close to forty years old, for God's sake.

Carl told me the other people working there used to laugh when she cozied up to him and flirted with him. They told him she was after him and he'd better give her what she wanted or else. They thought it was funny.

No one's really sure what happened. They tried to piece it together but they couldn't talk to Carl or the woman so who knows? What they *think* happened, and from what I know I have to go along with them, is that she waited until it was just the two of them in the restaurant—he was always the last one to leave at night—and then she made her move. They found her skirt and blouse on the floor by the office. She took them off there and then followed Carl into the bathroom. They said she followed him because there was...uh...urine on the wall and floor. She must have scared him while he was...you'd be scared too if someone busted in on you and all she was wearing was her underwear. So she's coming toward him and he's backing away, trying to zip himself up, looking for a way out, only she's between him and the door.

Now, you have to understand, Carl was a very mixed up boy. He'd had all these experiences and now here was someone else coming at him, tearing at his clothes.

What happened was he just snapped. I think if he'd had control of himself he would have stopped before it was too late. He hit her and hit her and then he dragged her into one of the stalls and jammed her head into a toilet. And that was that.

No, it isn't a very pleasant story.

Here's the most recent picture I have of Carl. I can't stand to look at it. That's not him. That's not the boy I knew. Those eyes aren't his. That ugly white face isn't his. It's someone else. Some madman, y'know?

## The Cattletruck

I watch as the child approaches, swaying and lurching down the aisle as she combats the car's tricky contortions.

She and I have been sneaking looks at each other since I was helped aboard by sickened porters several hours ago.

"Man, you sure in rough shape," one of my dark,

uniformed aides had mumbled.

I saved myself some pain by just nodding. The skin on my face is so tight that the slightest movement causes it to split open. Despite my efforts the blistered skin voids a good amount of purulent matter into the gauze wound about my head. The dried pus acts as a mortar, encasing my face in a painful *papier-mâché* mask.

There will be no relief forthcoming. The shortage of medical personnel means that I must travel alone, untended, forgoing luxuries like periodic changes of dressing. It will be a long, excruciating trip to...wherever. There is a large displaced persons camp out on the prairies but I hear food is short even in the breadbasket of the world.

*"Listen," the doctor insisted, "you can't stay here. We can't do anything more for you and we need the bed. It's a simple as that." I stared up at him. He kept his eyes on his clipboard as if reading from a prepared statement. "You must have someone, somewhere. Sisters? Brothers? They can take care of you. We're just overwhelmed, you understand?"*

*I turned my face to the wall.*

*"It says here you're from out west originally. Well, there*

*you are. They didn't get it too bad out there." He waited for me to say something but I wouldn't oblige him. "We...we'll keep you here tonight but tomorrow you'll have to leave. I'm sorry. And I want you to know I wish you the best."*

*I heard his shoes squeak on the gymnasium floor as he moved on, his arrival at the next cluster of patients greeted by cries of relief, pitiful pleas for morphine.*

*Don't ask for too much, I thought, because people who need too much—*

The train is slowing.

Immediately I recall the reports I've heard of the recent resurrection of a lost art: train robbery. Bands of people crazy with hunger are tearing up tracks, deliberately derailing trains, burrowing through the hissing wreckage for a morsel, a mouthful, anything to line their acidic stomachs with.

They might like me, I come pre-cooked, ready to serve.

The train picks up speed again and the part of me (it grows more persuasive each day) that wants all of this to be over is disappointed.

During my reverie the child has advanced a few more steps, her gaze frank and penetrating.

She is a little charmer, this one, her antics earning indulgent smiles from the adults around her. She's headstrong and determined to move about at will. Not shy either. I've enjoyed watching her but have dreaded the moment when her inquisitiveness drew her in this direction.

Somehow she has summoned the courage to shamble toward me—one finger tucked reflectively in her mouth—and for that she is to be congratulated. But I curse her too because I can picture the scene that is about to transpire: the little girl wailing and crying, her mother rushing to her side to protect her from the mangled boogeyman, the reproachful glares of my fellow passengers...*as if it's my fault.*

I shake my head.

She pauses.

I thrust out a wrapped hand, waggle it in a shooing gesture. The concealing mitten only further piques her curiosity. She takes another step.

I sigh.

She's close now, close enough to smell me. Her little nose wrinkles daintily. But she doesn't run away and doesn't scream or cry.

"You look...funny," she says.

And giggles.

The statement is so unexpected, so cogent, so anti-climactic that I have to laugh along with her, a sibilant wheeze escaping from between clenched teeth. Good laughter, not bitter. I welcome the pain that flushes my features.

"That's because I *am* funny," I grate, "the biggest joke of all."

"What do you look like, underneath all that gunk?"

"Funny," I shoot back.

She cackles. "I know, but what do you *look* like?"

I think about that. Recalling the poor souls pressed into service as assistants, orderlies, nurses and sometimes even surgeons in makeshift hospitals throughout the city. Men and women who had to maintain their composure no matter what, even as they cut away dressings and uncovered a person whose humanity had been distorted or even *erased* by fire or flying glass. A few revolted against the demands imposed on them by the carnage. A big fellow, over six feet tall and swollen with muscle, broke down as he removed the last layer of my bandages. He vomited all over the bedclothes, fell to the floor, where he proceeded to kick and flail at anyone who tried to restrain him.

*"He's a meatloaf!* A fucking meatloaf!"

How do I look?

"I look like...like there are big blobs of melted plasticine all over my face."

That earns me an "Ooooo." I see the little girl's mother preparing to rise from her position opposite a young couple. "You'd be great at trick 'r treatin', y'know," she advises me.

"Oh, yeah, I do it all the time."

"Really?" Her expression is dubious.

"Sure. Got some peppermints off this guy the other day." Actually, they've been in my pocket for ages. "Would you like to have one?"

"Sure!"

"Rachel?" Her mother is calling, craning her neck, trying to see the current object of her daughter's attention.

"In my coat," I urge her.

She's torn between obeying a parent and the promise of a treat. Finally, she moves closer, reaches into my pocket and removes the candy.

I expect her to retreat from me quickly but she lingers. She reaches down, strokes my wrist, my fingers, cradling my palm, careful not to press.

"Does it hurt much?"

"Oh...sometimes."

She draws the hand up, plants a placating kiss on the yellowed wrapping.

Hot and salty, the tears slip down my cheeks, emblazon a crooked path of pain to my chin.

Stinging.

Burning.

"RACHEL!"

Her mother wrenches her away, a swift, snatching motion that startles us both. Rachel begins to cry.

"I'm really sorry—"

"It's okay, she was just—"

"—won't happen again, I'll—"

"—really, we were only talking—"

"—for any inconvenience—"

"—please—"

The woman speaks to the conductor who helps her stuff

Rachel's toys into a shopping bag before escorting the two of them from the car.

My hands contract into tight, angry fists.

*I wasn't going to hurt the kid—*

I bring my hands up to my face, stare at them.

Until moments ago, charred tissue and soldered cartilage prevented all but the slightest movement of either hand. My fingers had been fused together, ensnared in a web of tough, violet flesh. I required assistance for the simplest tasks like zipping up my coat or using the washroom.

But now...

I open-close-open-close my hands. Marveling at the complexity of a universe that, despite the horrors lately inflicted, still offers the remote prospect of mercy to those who need it most.

# The Strange Music

"Okay," I heard dad say, "so it was a bad idea to go."

"Yes," she agreed, "a *very* bad idea."

And if I wasn't supposed to have been asleep I would have gone along with that myself. I was curled up under the coats in the backseat, breathing really deep and slow. But I was listening, and I had to listen hard because they were talking so softly, especially him. Dad never yells, even when he's giving you heck for something.

"It's going to be all right, Lorrie," he said but I could tell he didn't believe it and if I could tell—

"You're such a shit," she said, "such a fucking shit."

I think he said "okay" but I couldn't hear because of the noise the wheels were making. She gave a mean laugh and I started shaking because I've heard that laugh, plenty of times.

"I can't get their faces out of my head," she said, "all

those stupid, asinine faces. It was like I lifted up my skirt and pissed in the punchbowl." We hit a rough spot in the road. "— show them for laughing."

"No one was laughing," he broke in, "get that straight. No one was laughing."

"They were *laughing*," she insisted, "like a bunch of hyenas."

"Jesus Christ." He lit a cigarette and right away she opened her window so I snuggled deeper into the coats.

"Elizabeth is such a bitch."

"She is not a bitch," he snapped, "she's a good friend, she cares about you—"

She cackled again. "More like she cares about you. She's wanted into your pants for years."

"That's enough."

"Fuck her and her precious party."

I wanted to kill her then. For what happened at the party, for embarrassing us so bad and for what she was doing to him now. I could have told him it was no good trying to talk to her, no use telling her *please, please stop*. My back started itching. It always does when something bugs me.

"Why are you doing this? What sort of pleasure does this kind of—of assassination give you?"

"You've talked to the shrinks, kiddo," she said sweetly, "you should know by now. I'm a psychotic bitch. You should have me locked up. No one would blame you the least bit. Especially after my latest little performance. I think it was my best yet, don't you?"

"No," he muttered, "no, Lorrie."

"I hate you," she said. "I hate you and I hate little Pete and his blond hair and big, watery eyes and his stuffed walrus and if you ever leave me alone with him—"

"—no, no—"

"—do it again, only maybe this time you won't come home in time to..." I couldn't hear the rest because he was pulling over to the side of the road and stopping.

He was crying, bent over the steering wheel, twisting it so hard I could hear it squeaking between his fingers. My back was burning, I couldn't keep still. I sat up and she turned around and looked at me and I swear to God her eyes were shining.

"Wakey, wakey," she said and grinned at me and I

started hitting her, hitting her as hard as I could and she didn't do anything, just sat there and let me until dad grabbed my hands and pushed me back down onto the seat.

"See," I heard her say, "he's learning what it's all about. Welcome to the real world, sonny-boy."

"I HATE YOU!" I screamed. "I HATE YOU AND I HOPE YOU DIE!"

"Pete," dad whispered, "don't." He was trying to reach out and pinch my lips shut but she was holding on to his arm and grinning that crazy grin of hers.

"Let him go," she told him, "it's music to my ears."

*The End*

"...mmm?"

"Daydreaming again, I see."

"Can't help it. You know how it is."

"I know." She reached out, plucked at some invisible lint on the front of his shirt. Like a madwoman, he thought. And shuddered.

Someone knocked on the front door. "I'll get it," she offered. He nodded and went back to staring at the wall. She shuffled down the hallway, admiring the freshly washed walls and the floor she'd scrubbed twice today. She reached the door, opened it to a man who looked like a bank clerk.

"Mrs. Barker, my name is Myron Bryce and I work at the bank."

"Oh, how nice, won't you come in?" She stepped aside and he entered: a tall, thin, gawky-looking specimen with impeccably shined shoes.

"Thank you very much," he said.

"George," she called out, "the man from the bank is here."

"What? What was that, Ella?"

"There's someone from the bank here to see us," she repeated.

"What in God's name for?" They heard the sound of a chair scraping across the floor and footsteps coming toward them.

"Yes, I guess I should have wondered that myself," she said, cocking her head quizzically. "Now why on earth didn't it occur to me?"

"I...expect it's the—uh—circumstances of—uh—" Bryce broke off as George Barker came into view.

"What's all this about?" He demanded, stalking toward them. "Surely you must realize that my wife and I don't want to be bothered right now—"

"Of course, sir, of course I do," Bryce agreed, "but there's the matter of your loan..." The Barkers looked at each other, then at him. "The loan, you see," he persevered, "for your car.

You still have," he checked the folder he held, "just over eleven hundred dollars to pay on it. I was wondering, um, if we could clear this whole matter up, you know, just so the account's settled and—and all that."

There was a pause that just kind of hung there like a big, empty thought balloon, waiting to be filled.

"You must be mad," George snapped.

"I mean, *really*," Ella, his wife of thirty-six years, chimed in.

"I know this may seem, ah, strange and perhaps even in bad taste—"

"Yes," George said, "that's exactly how it seems."

"I can assure you that I don't feel very good about this either," Bryce confessed. "If you'll just give me a few moments of your time I'll have you sign the necessary papers and then you can write me a check for the amount owing..." Both husband and wife wore dismayed, angry expressions. "...don't you think?" He was perspiring, fidgety. Finding it difficult to meet their eyes.

"I don't believe this," Ella said.

"Well, I'm not going to stand for this impertinence."

George started back down the hallway. "I'm going to call the bank right now and give them a good—"

"There's no need for that," Bryce spoke up hastily. "That is to say, er…"

"What the dickens is this?" George stared the man down. "Are you from the bank or aren't you?"

"Well, yes…" The Barkers waited. "But I'm not here in an *official* capacity, you see. This is all…rather my own doing." Bryce seemed to be shriveling.

"So this is some kind of scam," George deduced, "some kind of last minute money grab—"

"No, no, not at all," Bryce demurred, "it's nothing like that." He sighed. "Oh, dear. I was hoping this would go much easier."

"Sorry to disappoint you," George retorted.

"George," she scolded, "don't be too hard on the lad." She patted Bryce's arm. "He's only trying to do his job, isn't that right, son?"

"Yes, ma'am," he said softly, "and I'm afraid I've made a botch of it."

"Now, now, don't be like that." Giving him a maternal

smile. "He has such a pleasant face, don't you think, George?" Even if he thought so her husband made no reply. "I'll bet you could use a nice cuppa tea right now, couldn't you, lad?"

He was caught off guard by the question. "Well, um, ah, sure, I guess. Yes, I think I'd like that very much."

"Why don't you go wait in the living room with George and I'll put a pot on. Go on now," a little nudge to get him started. He hesitated as he approached Barker, who gave ground, albeit reluctantly.

While the men waited they exchanged glances but no words. Finally she brought in a tray with a tea service and some biscuits. "Help yourself, lad," she coaxed, "they're not store bought, you know." He nibbled a biscuit while she poured.

"Delicious," he offered and she beamed at him.

"Yeah, all right, let's stop the chatter and find out what's going on here." George ignored her as she held out his cup so she set it on the coffee table in front of him. "Come on, lad, out with it."

"Don't be such a bully, George." She winked at the younger man. "Don't mind him, his bark is worse than his bite."

"Don't go on now, woman—"

"Mind your tone, George Barker."

"I'm just trying to find out—"

"Let him tell it in his own good time," she chided him, "that's good manners."

"*Hmmmppf*," her husband said, or words to that effect.

"Thanks very much, ma'am."

"Say nothing of it...um, Myron, wasn't it?" He nodded.

"Yeah, yeah, all right, *Myron*, so what are you doing coming around here bothering a couple of plain old folks like us, eh? For God's sake, man, why don't you leave us alone?"

"As I said, sir," Bryce glanced from one to the other, "I feel very bad about all of this, I really do. And I wish I'd had a chance to practice more—in all honesty, you're the first folks I've found at home. Or who've answered their door..." Tapping the folder beside his cup. "What, in effect, this *really* comes down to, in a nutshell, is putting your affairs in order and—and clearing the slate before...before..." But that was as far as he got. Something caught in his throat, caught...and held. The words would not come. It took his wits a moment to rally and during that interval there was the briefest glimpse of a spastic, pop-eyed, slack-jawed, drooling *thing* before Bryce reappeared, his mask of benign affability back in place. All of this happened in the space of a blink; if the Barkers saw anything it registered only subliminally, remarked upon by speckling of goose bumps.

"Surely you must see that paying off our car loan isn't the main thing on our minds right now," George said, rubbing his arms vigorously, wondering if he should knock the heat up a few notches.

"Yes, sir, I know but—" Bryce took another sip of tea. "I don't suppose you have a drop of something a wee bit stronger—"

"Haven't touched the stuff in eight years, eh, Ella?"

"And I'm proud of you, dear."

"Ah, never mind then." He took another sip.

"Come on, lad, out with it."

"I-I'm trying, sir."

"Of course you are." She patted his arm again. "Have some more tea. It's Darjeeling, you know."

"Wonderful stuff." Barker shifted impatiently, anxious for him to get on with his tale of woe and then get the hell out.

"I'm sorry, sir, I'll try to make you understand." Bryce mulled fretfully for a few seconds, then began his narrative with a soothing recitation of numbers. "I've worked at the bank for four years and seven months...as of yesterday as a matter of fact. And I've done pretty well for myself too. Started out as a teller, just like everyone else, but then I got promoted—a bit too quickly for some of the old hands, let me tell you. I don't think they were used to seeing someone with that kind of ambition and drive. I really love working at the bank, always had a head for figures, ever since I was a kid. I used to do my friends' math assignments, even stuff for kids in higher grades. Sometimes they paid me but most of the time I did it for nothing. *Hmm.* Sorry for going on like this," he apologized, "I know it must be a tremendous bore for you, listening to me talk about my job. Sure works with the ladies though." He smirked but no one got it.

"It's good that you like what you're doing. Not many people are that lucky, isn't that right, George? Mind, we were talking about this just the other day."

"*Mmmp*," he said.

"Go on, dear, tell us more."

"Might I...have another biscuit, please?"

"Certainly." She handed him the plate.

"And...is that jam?"

"Preserves," she corrected him primly. "My daughter makes them. She gives us some every time we visit her in the country. George, would you pass the jar, please?" At first he made no move to comply but, finally, under her hard gaze he relented, nudging the jar close enough for Bryce to reach.

"Well," he said, slathering his biscuit with sticky redness, "within three years I was assistant manager in charge of loans and then I applied for a job in Accounting. *That* raised some eyebrows. Nobody said anything but I could tell they thought I was making a big mistake. Nevertheless, I felt it was important that I keep working closely with numbers, that was my strong suit. To tell you the truth, I can't think of anything that makes me happier than tapping away at a calculator or computer all bloody day—excuse the French, ma'am. And the money's just as good so why not?"

"Accounting is a very good career, isn't it, George?" His answering grunt was inscrutable. "Yes, our Henry took classes for it at university but decided it wasn't for him."

"That was business administration he took," her husband said.

"Yes, but there was accounting involved," she replied. "Mind, George, it was me that helped him with his homework, not you."

"Not the same thing," he muttered.

"Was," she said.

"Wasn't," he *sotto voced*.

"What did he finally settle on...your son, I mean."

"Him?" Barker snorted. "He finally settled on being a bloody janitor—and *don't* bother excusing my bloody French."

She sighed. "This is an old wound, Myron." He nodded sympathetically as he engaged in a short scrum with George among the biscuits. "Our boy," Ella said, shooting a withering glance in her husband's direction, "he's a fine boy but he lacks..."

"Guts," George finished for her.

"Fortitude. That's the word." She nodded. "He can never seem to stay at anything long enough to make it work. He's not a ne'er do well or a bum or any of those other names George likes to call him. He's just kind of...*lost* right now."

"I understand," Bryce told her.

"Ha!" Barker said derisively. "Sure you do."

"Don't mind him. Go on with what you were saying," she urged him.

"There's not much more to add. I've been in Accounting and really loving it and there was an opening coming up because a chap was retiring and it would have meant..." He grimaced. "*Would* have meant a wage increase, perhaps even my own office. But now..." he set his teacup down, sat back in the chair, his face working nervously; and again both Barkers received fleeting impressions of a surging madness, seeking to break containment, bubbling closer and closer to the surface. "Jesus Christ Almighty," Bryce whispered. "It's really going to be over, isn't it? It's...oh, God...*God*..." His breath coming out in gasps.

"It's all right, dear," she said. "Have another cuppa."

"No," he said hoarsely, "I really shouldn't...I should be..." He swallowed a few times. "I must be moving on. I have other people I've got to see. I'm still only on the B's," he added wanly.

Barker was incredulous. "You mean you intend to go on

with this damn fool scheme of yours? Intend to keep bothering people in their misery just so you can balance your books?"

"I—I've got to," Bryce said. "I mean, just because of what's going to happen, just because no one else besides me had the, um, fortitude to show up for work, doesn't mean that it's right for me to neglect my duties." He stood up, retrieving the folder. "A man's got to do what a man's got to do," he pronounced, looking as silly as he felt.

"You're daft," Barker sneered.

"Sit down, dear," Ella told him. "Listen, do you have any people of your own?"

"Ma'am?"

"Do you have someone to be with when...well, when it happens? Because if you don't we'd be only too happy to have you stay with us, isn't that right, George?"

"What are you saying, woman?"

"Hush, now, I'm talking to Myron, aren't I?" She turned back to the accountant. "And you listen too, Myron. What George is saying...well, I hope you'll excuse me for saying so but I think he's right and you're wrong for doing what you're doing. All those figures, do you think they care one way or another what happens to them? I mean, they don't really *do* anything, they aren't going to suffer if you just leave them be." He frowned. "But, now, people on the other hand are different. People deserve a little more consideration than that, don't you think? Don't you think, Myron?" He bobbed his head once. "Yes, they do. Now, George and me, we're planning on listening to some old records, maybe seeing if there's anything on television and then later on we're going to drive out to visit Sarah, that's our daughter in the country. Henry'll be there too. Maybe the two of you can sit out on the porch, drink some beer and talk about numbers and...and things like that."

"Like mopping bloody floors and cleaning bloody toilets—"

"That'll be enough of that," she snapped and Barker clammed up. "He's our son and whatever he decides is all right with us. You *promised*, George," she reminded him. "You promised that no matter what you'd keep quiet. I intend to hold you to it." She turned back to Bryce. "What do you say, Myron? Would you like to stay with us? You're more than welcome."

"I really appreciate the offer, but..." He looked down at the folder. He looked at it for a long time. Finally he came to a decision. "Sure. Why not? I would never have gotten finished in time anyway."

"Good for you." She clapped her hands happily. Barker groaned and raised his eyes to the ceiling, praying for some kind of relief. Ella saw that Bryce was biting his lip, biting back a question that needed to be asked. "Is there something else?"

"Uh, Ella, there's this girl..." Blushing.

"Oh, yes," she said, with a knowing smile.

"She works at the bank and we've gone out a few times. Just for drinks and some talk, not much more than that." Shifting form one foot to the other. "She's really quiet and I don't think she has many friends. I was wondering—"

"Why don't you ring her up?" She suggested. "I'm sure Sarah won't mind a few extra guests."

"You're sure?"

"Of course," she insisted. "Oh, but the phones may not be working, you may have to drive over and ask her."

"I'll give it a try." He started toward the telephone. "Is it all right if I—"

"Go ahead, I'll put more tea on."

"Why don't you call the Queen and invite her along as well?" Barker growled. "And the rest of the Royal family while you're at it."

"I'll try, sir," Bryce promised, with a small, wry smile for Ella. "But you know how busy they usually are around this time of year."

"Smart ass," Barker rumbled. Ella shooed Bryce away and then began gathering up their dishes, stacking them on the tray, ignoring her husband's dour expression. He picked up the remote control, turned on the TV to get the latest news on the crisis. But as usual all he could find were exhortations from harried government spokespersons to remain calm and religious programs.

"I'll be glad when all of this is over," he muttered as he thumbed through the channels, alternately uplifted by promises of a better world to come and devastated by what was about to happen to the only world he'd ever known.

From the kitchen he could hear Bryce chatting on the

phone, to his lady friend presumably. What a travesty this day had turned out to be. He had hoped to spend what time Ella and him had left quietly, with no hullaballoo, but now all of that was just a lot of smoke. Ella was adamant they had to wait out the end of the world with Sarah the Nature Freak and Henry of the Lost Cause. And now she'd included this fool from the bank in their plans and his bird as well. What next?

"Ella," Bryce called, "Terry doesn't want to leave her dogs behind. Could we possibly—"

"Of course, dear, tell her to bring them along."

"*Now you lot wait one minute!*" George Barker roared, rising from his chair, standing in the middle of the living room, apparently the last sane person on the planet. "Is anyone around here listening to me?"

The madness continued, unabated.

After a time, no longer than a minute or so, Barker sat down and started staring at the far wall again, his gaze defiant, unwavering. Just because they had gone off their heads didn't mean *he* had to do the same.

No.

He would cling to his peace of mind and he would not let

go. Not for anyone or anything. He was going to hold on. He had to hold on. He held on.

# Snow Angels

She hasn't moved from the window since the storm started.

I come up behind her, slide a hand around her waist. Trying to break through the wall of isolation she's erected around herself, remind her that she isn't alone in her suffering, someone else grieves along with her. A futile gesture on my part. I should know better. I feel her shudder and withdraw my arm, giving her the space she clearly desires. I even pretend I'm not hurt, another act of consideration that goes unacknowledged; she hardly seems aware of me, her attention riveted on the swirling snow.

The forecast said the blizzard will last well into the evening. A front that originated in the Rocky Mountains, gathering momentum as it raced across the great plains. They're saying the airport might close; a lot of flights are being cancelled.

I hear myself speaking. "Honey, why don't you come away from there?" She doesn't blink or glance my way. "I'll fix you something to eat, how about that?" I wait a decent interval. "Hon? Did you hear what I said?"

"I'm..." As usual, her attempt at conversation doesn't go far. She lacks either the energy or interest to hold up her end of an exchange.

Suddenly, I'm seized by a desire, almost a *compulsion* to grab her, give her a good shaking, slap her until she comes around. Fed up with the zombie routine, needing my wife back, the person who once occupied that body. The woman I love.

But that isn't fair. Immediately I feel shame, regret. I'm tired, worn out, but that's no excuse. This is no time to be selfish and petulant. I need to be more sympathetic and attentive. I need to be her rock.

"Snowing pretty hard," I offer.

No reaction...and that's what hurts most of all. By closing herself off, refusing me admittance, she's denying us the chance to draw strength from each other, share our pain and perhaps come through this awful time together, intact. She can't see beyond her own agony and is unable to understand that *I* might be hurting too, in need of a word, a token expression of kindness or support. The merest touch of a hand...

The anger surging again. *Goddam you. Why don't you wake up and realize what you're doing to the rest of us—*

"I saw you...shovel the driveway." Wrapping her arms around herself. "You looked cold."

"I was. And now it's snowing even *more*, spoiling all my hard work." My voice sounds wrong. Toneless and robotic. Then it gets so quiet I swear I can hear the snowflakes hitting the window: *pht, pht, pht.* Evaporating almost immediately, leaving little evidence of their passing.

Suddenly she stiffens, leaning closer to the window. The snow and grey twilight making it hard to see. Another day on the wane, one more endured and crossed off the calendar. It has to be close to suppertime but neither one of us has much of an appetite, despite the food over-flowing the refrigerator or piled in the freezer. Lasagna and pot roast and fried chicken. Pies and pastries. Left by good, well-meaning people and bound to go to waste.

"Can I fix you something or—"

She gestures impatiently. "There's some kids out there."

"What?" I go to look but the cold glass fogs up on me. I swipe at it, creating a blurry mess. "They're probably on their way home from somewhere." I scan the vicinity, seeing nothing. "I don't—"

"It's two big ones and a little guy..." I heard her make a sound of alarm. "Oh, look, look...they're picking on him! One of them pushed him down—"

"Where—" The blizzard is messing with my field of view, obliterating everything more a few feet from the house.

"Over there by the street light. Oh, Kev, Kev, now they're throwing snowballs at him!" Finally turning to me, eyes wide and imploring. "We have to help him, go out there and—"

She must see something in my face, some flicker that gives away the game. I reach for her and she slaps at my hands. "Karen—"

"I see them I tell you! They're out there and we've got to do something!" Her face flushed. "Are you blind!" She points. "Look!" I won't. Can't. She brushes past me and before I can prevent her, she's pulling open the front door, inviting the blizzard into our warm, comfy house. "Hey! Hey, you, stop that!"

"Karen, for Chrissake!" By the time I reach her she's on the front step, no coat, no shoes, hollering to break up a fracas only she can see.

"Get away from him! Leave him alone!" When I tried to grab her and pull her inside, she balks, evading my hands and cursing my recalcitrance. "What are you doing? Why aren't you helping instead of—"

"Karen!" I shout, trying to snap her out of it. "Get inside! *Now*!"

She shrinks from me. "But he—he—"

"There's no one there! No one! You're just...it's all..." Where the fuck is Grimes when I need him the most? Grimes, with his silky, soothing voice and his pills, oozing reassurance and understanding. I lunge for her, snag an arm, start dragging her toward the open door. She resists fiercely, displaying surprising strength, seemingly oblivious to the subzero temperature and dire wind chill.

"Help him, damn you!"

We're in the doorway, she's twisting in my grip, but I pull her close, embrace her tightly. "He's dead, baby," I whisper, feeling my guts convulse as I say it, "dead and buried."

And that's when I hear it.

Borne on some directionless wind, inaudible to all but those who have suffered and endured too much...a voice, so tiny it should have been lost in that gale, a few short syllables that combine to deprive me of what remains of my sanity.

"...*cold...so cold...*"

Karen sees from my eyes that I've heard it too and for the first time in weeks she's smiling. "Go to him, Kev," she urges me. "Bring my baby home." Fetching my coat and boots from inside, helping me dress right there on the front step, urging me to hurry.

I descend the slippery stairs, drawing up my hood against the searing wind. The storm rushes forward to meet me. Head down, bent almost in half, advancing into the teeth of it, half-blinded by blowing snow and sleet.

Determined to follow that voice, wherever it might lead me.

## Sex * Tet: A Horrific Medley of Old Favorites

*Sleep/Benediction*

Sleep, I silently command, go to sleep.

I adjust my rearview mirror so I can watch the little boy in the back seat. His eyes slowly roll back. He fights it. But he's all whites and yawns. Finally, he succumbs, his head bobbing like one of those novelty dogs. I drive on, humming under my breath.

Will they have roadblocks up yet?

I want to turn on the radio, listen to the local news. But I don't want to wake the tyke up. Don't want him asking for his mommy and daddy again.

Sometimes it's hard to be hard.

Sleep, little one.

Sleep...and dream. Dream you're at home in your mommy and daddy's house instead of in a car with a monster, heading for his dark, secret lair. Take shelter in your dreams, child.

While you still can.

*God, I love you*

I wish I could split your head open like a watermelon, split it right down the middle. I'd love to have your brains puddling all over me. I'd love to be washed, *anointed* in your blood. I want to jump rope with your intestines, scratch my back with your pubis, pick my nose with your big toe. I'd love to fuck you up your cold, tight ass. I'd love to come as I sit on your moldering face. I'd shoot big gobs of jizz into your matted hair. And as I did, I'd be whispering over and over again:

God, I love you.

God, I love you.

God, I love you...

*If you could read my mind*

I remember thinking

I remember thinking

I remember thinking

It was during "The Avengers". We were watching the show and I thinking

*thinking*

Steed and Tara were making lovey-dovey eyes at each other and you were going on about how made up and phony she was and I said I thought she was sexy and you said I'd fuck anything in a skirt and smelled like fish and I was thinking

about a lot of things

about how ugly you were and how you'd let yourself go and how you used to turn me on so much and now you have piles and wear curlers and never want to fuck and I was watching Tara and

I was thinking

*imagining* what it would be like to be between her legs instead of yours and I was thinking about her and me and you and I started playing around with the belt of my housecoat, untying it and then reknotting it, untying and reknotting it and

I was thinking...

*Playmate*

Are you supposed to look vulnerable with your legs in the air, two fingers buried in your cooze?

Is that pouting expression supposed to make you look like a schoolgirl whose grades weren't as high as she expected?

In this shot, you're framed against an ascending (or descending) sun. Was that to give the impression of a halo?

Here you're zipping along in a fire engine red convertible, top down, hair streaming behind you.

This is a nice one: satin sheets and sleepy/sultry eyes. Is that airbrushing or is your complexion really that perfect?

Are you real or the artificial construct of some imaginative graphic designer?

I stretch out my fingers but instead of wet/warmth, I find gloss and pretension.


*Glory Days (Slight Return)*

"What's this one?" She asked, running one long, knowledgeable finger along a scar that horseshoed his left knee.

"Torn ligaments," he told her. "The pocket collapsed and I got sandwiched between two linemen. *Boom!* Last game of the season against the Steelers.

"And this?" Tracing a livid crosshatching on his thigh.

"That one came courtesy of Otis Washington, used to be a tackle for the Bills. Mean? Busted my damn leg and walked away laughing." He looked bemused as he lit a cigarette. "And that guy's bound for the Hall of Fame they say."

"How about this one?" Her fingers had moved to a ridge of scar tissue over his ribs.

"Blind-sided by a d.b. I think he played for the Browns. Or maybe it was the Bengals..."

"And...*this*?" She prodded an angry welt near his belly.

"You gave me that one," he reminded her.

"Yesss..." She moved over him, impaled herself with a quick, expert flick of his cock.

"Oh, babe," arching his back, "do it, do it..." She took the cigarette from him, held it to her thin, cold lips, sucked on it once, twice, savoring the moment while he sweated and twitched beneath her. "Please, baby, please—"

The cigarette dipped suddenly, searing a dime-sized

patch of skin on his chest. He bucked and jumped but she held on tight, clamping her legs around him, keeping him inside her.

The pain.

It brought to mind off tackle runs and collisions in the backfield and goal line stands and perfect spirals and Super Sundays and circus catches and Gatorade and cheerleaders and bloated, intense faces and packed stadiums and rabid crowds...sweet memories of yesterday's heroics, yesterday's victories.

"Ah," he breathed. "*Ahhhh...*"

"What?" She asked him. "What did you say?"

"Again," he whimpered, "do it again."


*The Joy of Necrophilous Bestiality*

And she says it's hopeless. And she gets dressed. And she leaves the bedroom. And you lay there in your own sweat. And you listen to her strangle the cat on the way out. And you twist the sheets, in the grip of an impotent rage. And you cry like a baby. And you scream for her to come back. And she drops the cat. *Thud*. And she closes the front door behind her.

And you get up. And you find the cat's body. And you pick it up. And you pet it. And you become aroused. And you take it back into the bedroom with you. And when she calls a couple of days later, you don't recognize her voice.

## Teenage Wasteland

*"I shall not repeat (Marco Polo's) story of the Old Man of the Mountain, who used to administer hashish...to his younger disciples when he wanted to give them an idea of paradise."*

—*The Poem of Hashish* by Charles Baudelaire
(Translated by Sallie Sullivan)

He was seventeen going on a hundred as he waited on the darkened doorstep.

He knocked again, harder this time.

"Come on, come on," he muttered.

Then the door swung open and there was Lloyd, ugly old Lloyd, sporting an illegal smile if he ever saw one.

"Heyyy, Jamie, c'mon in." He stepped inside, escaping the brooding twilight. "You wanna take off your shoes? I washed the floor this afternoon."

"Sorry." Jamie pulled off his huge Nikes, set them on newspaper with three other pairs of running shoes.

"Everybody's in here." Lloyd led him down a hallway festooned with posters of rock 'n roll icons—he called it the "wall of infamy"—and into the living room. Shaun, Lloyd's brother, had just popped Led Zeppelin's "Houses of the Holy" into the CD player.

The music helped. Some of the propaganda Jamie had been force-feeding his conscience began to sound pretty convincing. It's going to be all right, he reasoned. Nobody's going to get busted, nobody's going to knife me and take the money I earned working all those Friday and Saturday nights at fucking Dairy Queen.

"You already know Shaun. That guy over there," Lloyd pointed at the couch, "is the one, the only, Doctor Demento, the master of disaster, the sinister, the unreal, the supernatural, the super-human, the totally-awesome-out-of-this-world dope sucker himself...Lyle."

The man Jamie had come here to meet was in his early twenties. His seamless, adolescent face was plain, its features unremarkable, contours maddeningly vague. Though he was still a novice at the game, Jamie could see that possessing such a face had its distinct advantages. It was, he supposed, the perfect disguise.

Even though Lloyd had just made introductions, Lyle didn't offer his hand or say anything. He sort of gave Jamie the once-over; it was a casual perusal at best.

*Dick*, Jamie thought.

Shaun cranked the volume a bit more. "Listen to that," he urged, masturbating an invisible guitar.

"You wanna get high, amigo?" Lloyd asked him. "You can try some of the stuff you're buying."

"Sure." Jamie debated sitting on the couch next to Lyle but in the end chose the floor. "What do you think of it? Can you give it a rating?"

Lloyd laughed and looked at Lyle. "I can only say this: it really fucked me up. Need I say more?"

"Right on," Lyle murmured. Jamie didn't see his lips move.

"I guess that's as good a recommendation as I can ask for," Jamie commented.

"Don't worry," Lloyd said, giving him a thumbs up,

"you're definitely getting your money's worth."

"I don't sell shit," Lyle intoned from the couch.

"That's good to hear," Jamie said.

"These people," Lyle waved his hand regally, "these are good people, y'know? Excellent people. My kind of people." Jamie tried to look attentive. "They have good taste in music, they're generous...they make me want to do good things for them. Hey, have I ever ripped you guys off? Have I ever said no? Let you down even once?" The two brothers dutifully shook their heads. Lloyd caught Jamie's eye and smirked at him. "No way. Not me." Lyle looked at him. "I hear you're looking for two o-zees."

"That's right."

"I think I can help you out there."

"Great."

"—but...see, the thing is, the price I'm asking is pretty steep. Four hundred for two ounces. Best I can do."

Jamie nodded. "That's the price that was quoted to me."

"That's the price and if you wanna tell me to stick it, I'll understand. The town's pretty dry right now. I don't mind hoarding it for awhile."

"It just so happens," Jamie dug into his pocket, "that I have four crisp, new one hundred dollar bills right here." As he held them up he was thinking: well, that's that. Jesus, this is one of your humble servants. Please don't let my dad find out about this. Let me have the dope sold, the four hundred back in the bank, plus a few extra bucks for my trouble. If I can manage that in a week at the outside, I swear I'll read the Bible faithfully, try to make it to church more often, even sacrifice my firstborn child to you—JUST GIVE ME THIS ONE FUCKING BREAK!

When Lyle saw the money there was a flicker of interest, a tantalizing glimpse of inherent humanity. It was gone in a blink, quickly defaulting back to his normal, zoned out state. He slowly, almost reluctantly rose from the couch. "Would you care to step into my office?" Jamie and Lloyd followed him down the hallway to the kitchen. As the three of them sat at the table, Lloyd stuck a match to the joint he'd brought along. While Lyle rummaged through a white plastic grocery bag, Jamie toked up. The stuff smelled good and by the third or fourth hit, Jamie knew it *felt* good too.

"My compliments to the chef," he said in Lyle's general

direction.

The dealer wasn't listening. He was setting up a small, but elaborate scale. While Jamie watched from a nearby cloud bank, he meticulously weighed the dope.

"Okay?" Lyle asked.

"Looks fine."

"I don't want you thinkin' I ripped you off."

"Don't sweat it." Jamie handed him the joint.

"You want me to divide this into quarters for you?"

"That'd be great," Jamie said. "I was wondering how I was gonna manage that."

"If you're gonna deal, you gotta have a good set of scales."

"Huh-uh. This is meant to be a quick score, something to get me some fast spending money. My dad's got this Vulcan death grip when it comes to money. Every time I want to buy something it's always SAVE IT FOR COLEGE. Fuck, what am I supposed to live on *now*?" Lyle trimmed the buds with a small set of scissors.

"You think you can get rid of two o-zees that fast?"

"I *have* to. If my dad finds out what I've done, he'll cut

my balls off."

"You could say you were merely showing a healthy interest in the capitalist system," Lloyd kidded him, "trying to comprehend economics by becoming involved, goddamnit! What we're talking about here is fucking supply and demand, man. That's what the whole system operates on. That's it in a nutshell."

"I'll say it was a project for Social Studies. Along with, like, a thousand word essay—"

"—like when they make you write about 'How I Spent My Summer Holidays'—"

"—only this time it'll be 'How I Turned All Of My Friends Into Hopeless Junkies'—"

"—'And Made A Tidy Profit At The Same Time'!" Jamie and Lloyd yukked it up, flying high, getting off, but Lyle remained stiff, unsmiling.

"You guys sure talk a lot," he grunted.

"Hey, man," Lloyd said, "chill out. We're just baked."

"Shit," Lyle sucked the dregs of the joint. "This stuff doesn't do much to me any more."

"I don't know what planet *you're* from but us Earthers

are right fucked up, isn't that right, James?"

Jamie nodded, listening to his fingertips hum.

"That's okay for you guys but, me, I'm a connoisseur." Lyle dug into the plastic bag again, retrieving another pouch of dope. He threw it across the table to Lloyd. "Here. Roll us a nice joint out of that." Lloyd looked down at the baggie. Then he looked at Jamie and they both looked at it. The dope was black, jet black, and it appeared damp, like freshly turned dirt.

Lloyd picked up the baggie, opened it, stuck his nose in and took a whiff. Immediately he recoiled, dropping the baggie on the table with an exclamation of disgust. "Whoa, that's...Jesus..."

"What's wrong with you?" Lyle asked.

"What the fuck is that?"

"It's dope, best dope in the world—"

"It *ain't* dope. It smells like...I dunno, man, you smell it."

Jamie took the bag, sniffed tentatively, was assailed by a thick, rancid odor and he too thrust the pouch away. "He's right," he told Lyle, "the stuff's gone rotten or something. I wouldn't smoke this if I were you."

"What do you guys know? I'm telling you, you smoke this shit and you'll get off like you've never gotten off before."

"Yeah," Lloyd cracked, "I hear you get off pretty good when you die. I ain't interested in finding out for myself."

"Gimme that." Lyle took the baggie, peeled off a slip of rolling paper, peppered it with some of the black dope, rolled it into a neat, tight cylinder. "There's nothing like it in the whole world," he told them. He lit up, took a good, long hit. "Best shit ever," Lyle breathed, offered the joint to Jamie.

Jamie was already ridiculously high at that point and feeling cocky as hell so he took the spliff, gave Lloyd a shrug and *phhhhhhsssst!*

The stuff was wicked, harsher than the scummiest homegrown he'd ever smoked. It coiled and writhed in the back of his throat and Jamie suddenly pictured a cluster of larvae hatching in his mouth, white, bulbous, eyeless heads erupting from wet flesh; he almost gagged.

But it was dope, amazingly good dope, with a kick even harder than pure honey oil. It was bouncing around his skull, looking for the washrooms, finally giving up and pissing all over his cerebral cortex.

He handed the joint to Lloyd, who regarded it with distaste. "Good," Jamie croaked.

"Smells bad," Lloyd complained. He managed two quick puffs before he squeaked, shook his head and started hacking and coughing like a terminal case. Jamie laughed and laughed; Lyle favored them with a tight, absurd smile.

"Fuckin' guys," he said, starting another joint. "Keep smoking, pal," he advised Jamie. "Remember: too much reality can be detrimental to your health."

Jamie raised the joint to his lips. It took a long time to get there. As Lyle looked on he took three fast hoots, then one long, slow one before passing it to Lloyd.

"You got it. Yeah," Lyle said. "You're a big boy now. On the A-Team."

"Right on," Jamie said.

"Now you know why I call this stuff Oblivion," Lyle took the spliff from Lloyd. "This shit'll take you there. Never-Never Land."

A couple of years later someone remembered Shaun. Lyle rolled another joint of Oblivion then carefully, reverently sealed up the baggie. They walked into the living room in time to catch the opening riffs of Pink Floyd's "Comfortably Numb".

They knelt in a circle, passed "Oblivion" around like a holy relic, each of them sharing a moment of intimate communion with it before reluctantly surrendering it to the next pilgrim. And the music was like a chorus of angels, even when it turned on them with a snarl, sawing into their guts, ripping glistening coils of intestine from their stomachs, hollowing them out like Halloween pumpkins.

Jamie felt nothing. He was past the point of no return and saw no road signs indicating the way back. He decided to hang on and hope for the best. But the thing he was riding didn't want to be rode and more than once he ended up flat on his back, staring up at the ceiling. He heard someone laughing. He didn't care. Nice ceiling. He walked around on it for awhile, scuffing chunks of plaster on to their heads. No one seemed to notice so he gave up and swung down. He skulked about looking for something to munch on, then thought "fuck it" and headed off in search of a 7-11.

He did all of that without moving a muscle.

This is very bad, he thought. He wondered if the others

were tripping out like this. He bugged his eyes out at them. *Well?* But they didn't seem to notice. Or maybe they were ignoring him. Should he be getting pissed off?

He had to breathe with his mouth open, that was important.

He resolved that if he lived through this he would definitely buy a quarter of Lyle's fucked up dope. Then he came to the conclusion that reality was prejudicial to the norm and just as quickly forgot about it. The meaning of life is irrelevant. Be a seeker of truth of the highways and byways of vigilance...and don't drive drunk.

WHAT?

Jamie shook his head. He was convinced he was having some kind of stroke or aneurism. Every so often he'd get a jolt, this *rush,* and everything would collapse in on him and he'd feel like he was suffocating. Total paralysis. Higher brain functions short-circuiting.

Bzzz bzzz bzzz

Something was nudging him. It was the Lyle-thing. "Wannanotherone?"

"Ah...ah..."

"Do you? Here." Another joint. Jesus, when would it end?

For awhile it seemed like it never would. The music played on and on; time meted out in four or five-minute increments. The Doors. Blue Oyster Cult. Sabbath. Iron Maiden. AC/DC.

It was during "Back in Black" that Jamie realized he was capable of coherent thought again. He could raise his head. Manipulate his fingers. Blink.

He checked his watch. Nearly midnight. Unbelievable.

Time sure flies here in the Twilight Zone.

Shaun got up, stretched, announced that he was heading to bed. Lyle gave indications he was preparing to leave.

"Wow," Jamie said to him, "that sure was some wicked dope, bro."

"No shit," Lloyd concurred, "fuckin' near blew my head off."

Lyle shrugged modestly. "Glad you liked it. I like to initiate people every so often. Good people."

"You—ah—wouldn't want to sell any of—" Lyle was shaking his head.

"No can do. There are very limited quantities available and I'm a greedy kind of guy. I'm willing to give you a taste every now and then but that's it."

"C'mon, Lyle," Lloyd whined, "lay a couple of doobies on us, for old time's sake."

Lyle kept shaking his head. "Nope. Besides," he said with a half-assed grin, "I'm not sure you can handle it."

"Are you kidding? I've done acid, mesc, DA, even that shit that guy sold us. Remember?" This directed at Shaun. "We thought it was angel dust only—"

"This is different," Lyle insisted. "Don't tell me it didn't feel different to you. You never smoked anything like that before."

"No, but—"

"But nothing." Lyle's face was animated now but...by what? Fear? Anger? Scorn? "Oblivion is bad medicine. Habit-forming. If I gave you a couple of joints you'd smoke them tonight and don't tell me you wouldn't 'cause I know you. And then you'd come around asking for more. I've been smoking dope since before you were born but I still have a helluva tough time controlling myself, holding off harvesting my plants before they're ready—"

"You grow it yourself?" Jamie asked.

Lyle looked nervous. "Yeah. Well, just Oblivion. It's sort of a...secret recipe, I guess you'd call it."

"*Wha-a-at?*" Shaun was skeptical. "Hey, dude, it's just dope. You can only grow it so many—"

"IT'S NOT JUST DOPE!" Lyle's fervor startled them. "It's..." He rubbed his face. "Okay, I guess I'm fucked up enough to let you in on my secret."

"A drumroll please," Lloyd quipped.

Lyle glared at him. "I grow it myself, yeah. I started as a kind of experiment. About...I dunno, a year ago...no, longer than that. It's not important. Anyway, I bought this really good grass off a guy. He said it was Thai, I dunno, maybe it was. It was so good I thought, hey, I'm gonna try growing some of this shit. I've tried a couple of times but the quality was never that good. I decided to give it one more try with these seeds." The smug look on Lyle's face was making Jamie uneasy. He had a feeling he wasn't going to like what he was about to hear. "I took extra care with this batch. I bought a big plant pot and found some lights at a garage sale." Shaun yawned into his fist. "I needed some dirt, some really good dirt that had lots of nutrients and stuff in it. I was gonna buy potting soil—potting soil for pot, right?—but then one day it hit me like a shot. I told myself, stick to the natural stuff, man, don't go for no store-bought substitutes. Now ask yourself: where's the best dirt in the world, got lots of fertilizer, plenty of good, organic ingredients—"

"A farm," Lloyd suggested, stating the obvious.

"No, man," Lyle said, waiting a half-beat before delivering the punch line, "a *graveyard*."

"...graveyard..." Lloyd repeated.

Jamie thought about the color of the dope, the smell, the...taste.

"Yup," Lyle bobbed his head. "I figured, hey, the dirt there's gotta be chock full of all the stuff plants need. And I was right! The very first seeds I planted grew into these beautiful, bushy plants. And the dope..." His eyes rolled. "Fantastic. Like...well, you guys know what I'm talking about." Grinning slyly. "There. Now you know my secret. Is that freaky or what?" Without waiting for an answer he headed off to the kitchen to collect his things.

After he left the room the three of them glanced at each other. No one could think of anything to say. Shaun finally made everyone grin when he twirled a finger beside his head. Jamie nodded somberly.

Jamie's eight quarters lay in a neat stack on the table. Weighed and bagged.

"You got something for him to put it in?" Lyle asked Lloyd, who speedily produced a brown lunch bag that did the trick.

"Did I give you—" Jamie started going through his pockets.

"Already taken care of," Lyle assured him.

Jamie couldn't remember giving him the money but it was gone so...

Lyle seemed a bit addled as he left. He kept checking to make sure he had his keys and his dope and mumbled about how he'd ridden his bike over and now, shit, *it's gotten so late and my bike doesn't have any of those reflector things*—

Jamie could tell he was angling for a ride but the idea of being trapped in a car with the irrepressible Lyle Q. Fucked didn't exactly make his liver quiver or his dong long. So he didn't say anything.

Finally, after a lot of stalling and the inevitable soul brother handshakes, Lyle literally stumbled out the door.

"That guy is a fucking wing-nut," Shaun declared, once he was gone.

"He's harmless," Lloyd said but he didn't look so sure. "Just a bit of a flake."

"I'm with Shaun," Jamie spoke up, "I think he's nuts. That shit about the graveyard and the dirt—"

"He was fucking with you," Lloyd said.

"He did a good job." Jamie's stomach was churning.

"Forget about it." Lloyd feinted a slap at his head on the way to the sink but Jamie didn't react to it. "Even if he did get dirt from a boneyard, what difference does it make? A friend of mine grows pot in pigshit. Disgusting, huh? Tell me what the difference is." Pouring himself a glass of water.

"I'm not sure," Jamie said. "All I know is that I'm not feeling too good right now." He pulled out a chair, sat with his head down.

"You're not going to power-puke or anything, are you? 'Cause like I told you, I just washed the floor."

"Can I get some water? I gotta get this taste out of my mouth." Jamie emptied the glass in a couple of gulps but it didn't do any good. He shook his head, signaling Lloyd for a refill.

"Forget it, I'm telling you," Lloyd said, moving to comply. "Think about all the money you're going to make on this deal. You could sell it for, say, seventy a quarter...but you'd be smarter if you sold it by the gram...say ten bucks a gram, fifteen if you're really greedy."

"But if I sell it in larger amounts I'll be able to get rid of it quicker."

"But you'll make a lot less money," Lloyd argued. Jamie twitched his shoulders. "Well, it's up to you."

"Can you put out the word for me? Be careful, y'know, but let people know I've got some if they're looking."

"Sure, no problem," Lloyd agreed. "Of course," he continued, "since I'll be acting as your agent you'll have to make it worth my while..."

"Jesus, are you ever a prick, Lloyd," Shaun observed.

"No, man," Jamie said, "he's right." He rolled a good-sized joint from his stash, handed it to Lloyd. "A down payment."

"Thanks. I always like a nightcap before I turn in.' He lit up. "Ah..." Then Jamie took it and bore down hard, drawing in so much smoke his eyes watered. "You're turning into a real dope fiend," Lloyd told him.

Jamie let the smoke out slowly. *Fuck. Shit. Piss.* That taste wouldn't go away. It clung stubbornly to the back of his throat, tickling his gorge. He helped himself to another glass of water.

Then he was high again. But, he thought, this is nothing like Oblivion. This is a silly, frivolous sort of high. Like you're drunk, only smarter.

He left soon after the joint was finished.

"Thanks a lot," he said to Lloyd as he tied his runners.

"No problemo," Lloyd grinned, "I really dig the commission."

Then he found himself outside, alone, in the possession of two ounces of marijuana with a firm intention to traffic. The long, dark street loomed before him like a cell block and his every step was remarked upon by prying, preying eyes. By the time he got to his car, he was a nervous wreck. He popped in a *Rush* CD but Geddy Lee's screeching had him thumbing "Eject" within a few seconds. He drove home slowly, both hands on the wheel, an ordinary, law-abiding citizen in every respect. He even wore his seatbelt.

He pulled into the driveway, cut the lights (check), engaged the emergency brake (check) and made sure the keys were in his pocket and *not* in the ignition (check).

As soon as he heard the television droning downstairs he knew he'd made it. He went into his room, locked the door behind him.

Yeah!

He dragged a chair over to one wall, climbed up, pushed a ceiling tile out of place, put the dope up there. Then he let the tile fall back. Perfectimundo!

Brushing his teeth and gargling helped, but the vestiges of Oblivion remained. He began to wonder if he would ever be rid of it.

He went downstairs and spent a few obligatory moments with the folks. He supplied them with a largely fictitious account of his evening then had a brief "discussion' with his father. Actually, his father did all the talking and he just stood there and went "yes, sir" every once in awhile. But it wasn't so bad this time because they were trying to watch some kind of nature show on PBS. Another one of those programs about how humans are screwing up the environment and killing a bunch of innocent animals in the process. His folks loved stuff like that. Once they got around to showing oil-slicked sea otters, Jamie stood up, mumbled "Night, everyone" and beat a hasty retreat upstairs.

He flopped on to his bed, mashing his hot face into the cool pillows. His head felt like it was overflowing and at first he didn't think he was going to be able to sleep.

But he did.

And he had this dream.

In the dream, he was Tony Montana, that guy Al Pacino played in "Scarface". He was a made dude. He had it all. Drugs, money, women, guns. Only he knew it wouldn't last. And he knew that when the end came it would be swift and terrible. And he knew that for his sins he would burn in the fires of hell for all eternity. And for a fraction of a second— that was how long it took to escape the soul-piercing pain into fuddled wakefulness—Jamie felt those flames upon him, felt his flesh melt away and his essence spill out and he saw that it was *black...*

## Public Enemy

Reflected on the inside of my dark sunglasses are my eyes.

Reflected on the inside of my eyeballs is my brain.

My brain.

My fine, young brain.

Amid those whorls and coils are memories of things past, perceptions of things present and forecasts of things to come.

It is a good brain and it has served me well.

A lot of people wouldn't respect my brain.

They would call it "criminal", prone to radical thoughts and dangerous permutations.

They would want my head and the brain inside it.

My parents tried to ruin my brain, programming it with

gibberish they didn't understand but adhered to anyway.

When I resisted their dictums, they beat me. When I cried in pain, they ridiculed me. When I grew older and tried to correct their faulty programming, they disowned me.

Of course, they weren't the only ones attempting to mold me.

The teachers were inept and there were too many of us for them to bring their full powers of persuasion to bear. The forces of "law and order" were more scattered then, less organized (and aggressive). Not like today. These days, police are well-trained, highly motivated and, more than anything else, *loyal*, eager to carry out the orders of the *junta*. They crack skulls, they kill, they torture and maim...and do so with impunity.

It is the politicians I hate the most. They put caramel-coating on shit and sell it to the most cynical constituent. Draconian laws are camouflaged in verbose language, while bills concerning human rights trail dull strings of subsections and qualifications.

Most are fooled into thinking the laws binding and gagging them are fair.

Thus, democracy has misled the "free" for hundreds of years.

The ideals are grand but the men and women interpreting them are motivated by selfishness and greed.

Prerequisites for holding office.


What makes my brain so different and why is it capable of resisting all their attempts to indoctrinate me?

I don't kid myself I'm special. I'm not.

I think it's because I've never believed in *anything*. Not Santa Claus, not the Easter bunny, not Christ, not Hitler, not Lenin—you see, I've never met them. To me, they're only symbols and symbols (as any damn fool knows) can be manipulated.

So how can I believe in them? (Note: even as a child I thought this way!!!)

How can you believe in something unless you can reach out and touch it, hold it in your hand?

I see with my eyes: but there are illusions that can fool the sharpest eyes.

I hear with my ears: but in a thick fog sounds can seem to originate from every direction.

I can taste: but the most virulent poisons are tasteless.

I can smell: but a human's sense of smell is nothing compared to a dog's.

But if I can *touch* it: then I know what I'm touching has substance. It is REAL.

Reality is important.

Reality can give comfort.

Reality can kill.

Illusions only delude.

I renounce all data brought to my fine, young brain that cannot be confirmed by my sense of touch.

Most of the time I keep my eyes closed. That's why I wear the dark sunglasses. People get disconcerted talking to someone who isn't looking at them. So I give them the illusion of attentiveness and it is *they* who are deluded.

Does that make me a hypocrite?

Maybe I've come to realize that only by playing their game can I hope to defeat them. (There! I've admitted my designs! Let them do their worst!)

Their eyes tell them I am docile, harmless.

Their ears cannot detect seditious comments.

They cannot taste or smell hate.

But...if they touched me...they would discover I'm trembling, throbbing with pent-up frustration and rage.

*Then* they would know.


None have gotten that close.

I am a conspiracy of one.

# Dry

A maroon, '98 Crusader was making its way down the narrow country road, a long plume of dust trailing behind it like a sooty, brown shadow.

Nathan Dawes was ensconced behind the wheel. He was a man who might be described as pleasantly plump; his belly wasn't big enough to be an indictment of his eating habits...not yet anyway. The effusive heat had him gushing perspiration, his shirt slicked to him like another oily layer of skin. He wiped at the streamers of salty sweat that burned his forehead and cheeks and uttered a few hoary curses in the direction of the evil, blighted soul who'd assigned him a vehicle without functioning air conditioning. For the umpteenth time he glanced at the temperature gauge, which had been creeping into the red for the past half hour. The car feeling the effects of the blazing hot summer day even more than he was.

He spied a mailbox ahead and eyed it hopefully but when he drew abreast of it he saw that the stenciled name was "A. Henderson". Not his man. He gnawed fretfully on his lower lip.

Have to find the place soon or I'll be walking, he thought. Wonderful. It had to be at least a hundred out there. He stuck his left arm out the window—the wind rushing past was as hot as dragon's breath. A light on his dashboard began to wink ominously.

Another mailbox was coming up on the right. He squinted at it but, again, was disappointed. Dawes thumped the wheel in frustration. At that moment the front of the Crusader dipped into a sizeable pothole and he heard a thump as the bottom scraped on the gravel roadway.

"Stuck in the middle of nowhere," he groaned, visions of squashed oil pans dancing in his head. He turned on the radio but as usual all he could find were a couple of stations playing one country and western croaker after another:

> *"Oh, ma gurl done left me alone and blue*
> *What, oh, what, Lord, will I doooo..."*

He hurriedly turned it off, directing his attention to the land on either side of the road. It reminded him of photographs he'd seen of the split, corroded surface of the moon. A filigree of deep cracks cross-hatched the brittle ground, a kind of grim calligraphy etched by Mother Nature.

And the meteorologists continued their gloom and doom forecasts and the ozone withered away and the Greenhouse Effect intensified...

As Dawes looked on, a dust devil a hundred feet high careered across the field, plucking up any loose topsoil it came into contact with, bearing it away to parts unknown.

He was so intent on watching the mini-cyclone that he almost missed the turnoff. At the last possible moment he caught a peripheral glimpse of another mailbox. He braked sharply, craned his neck, read the name:

H. McCarthy

"Gotcha," he muttered, backing up a few yards and turning into the lane.

He drove slowly—the lane was in worse shape than the

road. Twice he debated getting out and walking but each time decided to proceed, wincing whenever the chassis rasped on the ground. Finally, he was out of the worst of it, pulling into a yard that fronted a small, well-kept farmhouse.

Over by the obligatory red barn a man who looked sixty and who was probably forty withdrew his hands from the guts of a partially disassembled tractor, wiping the gore on the front of his overalls as he studied Dawes.

A woman came out of the house, stood on the porch, her expression apprehensive.

He kept them waiting as he stuffed file folders and manila envelopes into his sun-bleached briefcase, sweeping all the paper cups and junk food detritus on to the floor. Once his affairs were in order, he took a deep breath, pushed open the door and stepped out.

The glare was incredible; it set fire to the top of his head and the back of his neck. His pupils shrank to pinpoints, he blinked rapidly, felt an ache begin behind his eyeballs, an ache that would soon invade every nook and cranny of his skull. Still, he put on his happy face as he ambled toward the house.

"Afternoon, ma'am." She nodded brusquely in his direction, looked over at her husband. Dawes followed her gaze, raised a hand in greeting. "You're Mr. McCarthy? Mr. Hal McCarthy?"

"That's right," the man confirmed.

"The name's Dawes, sir, Nathan Dawes. I'm really pleased to make your acquaintance." He turned back to the woman. "Ma'am, I wonder if you'd consider it an imposition if I was to ask for a glass of water. My throat feels as dry as the Sahara right now."

She opened her mouth. And closed it.

"Go get him one," McCarthy told her. "Looks like he could use it." She went inside and he came over and sat on the front step.

The years had been unkind to Hal McCarthy. His face was blanched and raw from constant exposure to the beleaguering sun. His shoulders were stooped from overwork, his hands thick and blunt and scaled by layers of calluses. Startlingly blue eyes looked out at a world that was increasingly hostile to those who stubbornly persisted at trying to eke out a living on the family farm. He looks wrung out, Dawes thought, wrung dry, like his land.

"Thanks for the water," Dawes said sincerely. "I know it's a mighty scarce commodity around here."

"Forget it."

McCarthy's wife came out, handed Dawes a glass. He smiled gratefully at her, tried to make eye contact, but she was too skittish, quickly relinquishing her hold on the glass and retreating. Dawes took a long swallow, draining half the water from the glass. "*Ah*. That's good. That's very, very good."

McCarthy glanced up at his wife. She shook her head at him but he just looked away. She stood by the door with her hands tucked in her pockets, somehow managing to look dignified and self-conscious at the same time.

"Hot day," Dawes said, to dispel the lingering silence.

"Yep," the farmer acknowledged. Then, after exchanging another meaningful look with his wife: "But no hotter than most around here."

"That's what I hear," Dawes said. "Boy, it must be tough on you people. How long has it been since there's been any precipitation?"

"Had some rain in early March," McCarthy recalled. "Lasted almost ten minutes," he added bitterly.

"How much snow did you get last winter?"

"Oh, yeah, *snow*." McCarthy snorted. "The fields were completely bare by January, isn't that right, missus?"

For the first time she spoke. "Like last year."

"Yep," the farmer said, "and the year before."

"That's tough," Dawes said.

"Mister, it don't get any tougher." McCarthy turned to his wife. "Watching Mr. Dawes drink has made me thirsty. Could you get me some water, hon? Lots of ice, okay?" She seemed reluctant to leave them alone. Finally, she went inside, the screen door snapping shut behind her.

"Well, sir," McCarthy offered as a preamble, "I guess we'd better get down to business before you melt."

Dawes drank the rest of the water, set the glass on the porch. Opening his briefcase, he retrieved a file. As he was checking it over, Mrs. McCarthy reappeared with an identical glass for her husband. McCarthy seemed distracted as he took it from her.

Dawes would have preferred doing business inside, out

of the heat, but neither of them made any overtures so he started his spiel. "I came, of course, in response to your application, which our office received ten days ago." He scanned the photocopy. "Everything seems to be in order." Glancing up at them. "I'm sure you both realize what a big step this is. However, if you are having second thoughts, if you'd like to go inside and talk this over, I'd be glad to—"

"We've already talked about it," McCarthy broke in, "talked about it 'til we're blue in the face. The time for talk is over." She was wringing her hands, squeezing and twisting them, trying to throttle the jabbering, capering things her emotions had loosed inside her.

"You're *sure*?"

"Look, Mr. Dawes..." McCarthy was exasperated. "Don't be trying to talk yourself out of a commission. It wouldn't do you any good anyway. All I need to convince me is to take a walk in one of my fields, pick any you please. You must have noticed them on the way here." Dawes nodded. "I had an old Indian guy out here last week, claimed he was some kind of medicine man. He said for fifty bucks he'd do a rain dance for me. I said 'okay, but no rain, no money'. He danced around the yard for a couple of hours, nearly got heatstroke. Nothing. Not a drop. As he was packing up he told me that his gods didn't think much of white men. I guess—I guess I can understand that." He drank some water. She came over and sat down on the step beside him but his pride prevented her from touching him.

"It could get better, y'know," Dawes pointed out. "The skies could open up any day—"

"Mr. Dawes, excuse me for saying so but you don't know what the hell you're talking about." McCarthy indicated the smoldering, relentless sun. "It's been almost four years now since any decent rain. Every once in awhile we get a sprinkle but there's so little of it that it makes me feel like God is...spitting in my face."

"Hal," his wife said, "Mr. Dawes is trying to be nice."

"I know it." He managed a wan smile. "I know he wants me to be sure." He gazed at Dawes. "I saw what you people did for Pete Gruber last year. While the rest of us were plowing our crops under and taking government handouts, he was bringing in a bumper crop." He paused, then the rest of it came out in a resentful jumble. "I've waited, hoped for rain, *prayed* for it...nothing. The bank has held off and held off, given me every break they can but they want their money and one way or another they're gonna get it." In spite of his predicament, McCarthy's expression and demeanor were defiant; he would bend but he would not break.

Dawes had heard variations of the speech many times before. Still, he found McCarthy's grim-faced depiction of reality affecting. He nodded slowly. "All right, sir, I've discharged my moral responsibility, I guess we can get down to business." She put her hand on her husband's shoulder. It wasn't difficult for Dawes to interpret the unspoken paragraphs inherent in that touch. "The contract itself is pretty straightforward. No fine print or sub-clauses." He placed a single sheet of paper on the hood of the car. McCarthy got up, came over and examined the sheet. After he read it through, he gave curt nod, signifying his compliance. "You're absolutely certain you wish to do this?"

"Yeah," McCarthy said softly. Resignation had dulled those blue eyes, stolen their luster.

Dawes took a small packet out of his pocket, extracted a shiny sliver of metal. "If you'll just hold out a finger..."

McCarthy looked back at his wife. She was standing now. Dawes was shaken and somewhat embarrassed by the emotion she exuded but McCarthy appeared unmoved. The unspoken plea evoked nothing but a flat, bland pronouncement:

"The land." He held out a grimy digit and Dawes pricked it with the pin. He guided the farmer's hand down to the page, smeared a droplet of blood across the dotted line.

"That's it?" McCarthy asked, his voice husky.

"That completes the transaction." Dawes placed the sheet in its proper folder, returned it to his briefcase.

"May God forgive me," he heard Hal McCarthy whisper.

"It's not as bad as all that," he commiserated. "I know you feel...empty at first. Don't worry, you get used to it." The expression on McCarthy's face was bleak. "You've done the right thing," Dawes assured him. "You've saved your farm, your way of life—" He saw that the farmer was deriving no comfort from his words, shrugged diffidently. "Well, I won't take up any more of your time, folks. I now you've got a lot of work ahead of you." As he opened the door of the Crusader, McCarthy spoke up.

"How soon before I—I see results?"

Dawes tossed the briefcase on to the passenger seat, settled himself before the steering wheel. "Almost immediately," he replied, glancing up at the burning sky. "I think you'll find that our people work pretty fast."

He waved to them as the Crusader pulled away.

McCarthy stared at the tiny hole in his finger. Behind him he heard the screen door shut with a hard slap. He could picture her standing at the sink, bawling, thinking him ten different kinds of fool for what he'd done.

Well, no use crying over spilled milk.

As he started back toward the house, a reassuring lie poised on the tip of his tongue, the world turned grey and the temperature dropped. He looked up and saw that the sun was hidden behind the biggest, blackest cloud he had ever seen. Over to the west, a second was materializing and to the north another huge bank. They defied the wind, defied nature, came together, clashed, merging into a mighty, coal-black phalanx that bristled with blue-white bolts of lightning.

Not long afterward came the first low rumble of thunder and as he listened to it roll it wasn't hard for Hal McCarthy to imagine some jealous god up there, growling in disapproval.

## Old Friends

"Hullo, Timmy! Hullo, Bruce!"

"Hi, Mr. D!" The two boys yelled, running over to greet him.

"Well, well, it seems my two old friends have missed me." The tall man grinned at each of them in turn.

"We sure did," Timmy said, reaching into one of Mr. D's pockets and taking out a *Snickers* bar (his favorite). Bruce was similarly rewarded with a rattling packet of *Glosette* raisins.

"And what have you been up to since the last time I dropped by?"

The boys took turns reciting a litany of juvenile preoccupations: baseball games, water balloon fights, mean teachers, embarrassed references to girls...

The tall man listened patiently until the account wound

down; then he straightened, his face set and serious. "That's *all*?" He demanded, his tone incredulous.

Both boys looked chagrined.

"Well..." Timmy began.

"It was fun," Bruce finished, looking like he wished he was somewhere else.

"Yes, yes, all right, it was fun," the man snapped, "but was it *daring*? Was it *dangerous*? Did you risk life and limb?" Timmy and Bruce looked at each other, then shook their heads. "Oh, dear," Mr. D frowned, "I'm afraid I'm very disappointed with you." The treats disappeared, even the stains of melted chocolate on their fingers fading away. The air around them got colder...and colder...

"We tried, honest we did," Bruce said, his voice cracking as it rose, "but it's hard coming up with stuff—"

"*Don't you have a garage, boy?*" Mr. D boomed and every bird within six blocks of them took flight. "You could be tying your mom's best towel around your neck and jumping off the roof like Superman." Seizing them by the shoulders, his grip strong enough to make them whimper. "You could be playing chicken on the railroad tracks or exploring that old grain elevator on the edge of town or teasing Gord Kurvers' Doberman. And what about checking out the old Shannon place—isn't it supposed to be haunted? You could go to the town dump and hunt rats, you could—oh, boys, boys, the list goes on and on." Mr. D's arms settled about them, drew them in closer. They could see themselves reflected in his glittering eyes and when he spoke, his voice seemed to come from everywhere. "You can *do* anything, *be* anyone you want. And you'll never die. You know it. So, you see," he said, smiling with those narrow lips of his, "there's nothing to be afraid of. Play and play and play...while you still have time," he added ominously.

When he pulled back, he saw from their expressions that his efforts had borne fruit.

"The river—"

"—remember we—"

"—gonna build a raft—"

"—like Huckleberry Finn—"

"—where we can get some boards—"

"—my dad's saw—"

He left them making plans for their next great adventure, whistling as he continued on his way, stopping now and then to exchange words with someone who recognized him but couldn't quite place the name.

## *"Live! From Planet Earth!"*

—Yes, that's right, gentle beings, another blockbuster episode of "Mass Destruction, Devastation, Mayhem and Good Clean Fun". Brought to you by Zoon's Ribbed Contraceptives. *Zoon's: all shapes, all sizes, all species.* I'm your host, Thrax, and, as usual, I am joined by Blom, who handles color commentary. Greetings, Blom!

—And to you, Thrax! As you know, I've been looking forward to this little skirmish for along time and I'm sure I'm not the only one who's been keeping his eyestalks on this remote but comely blue-green world.

—I think it's safe to add that the fact that old time nuclear weapons are being utilized by both sides only serves to heighten your anticipation.

—Absolutely, Thrax. Nukes are messy things that promise delightfully gruesome results. I remind you of the spectacle we witnessed last year on Trancha, a brutal slugfest involving—

—Sorry for cutting in but I believe we're just about ready to get things underway, Blom. Our cameras are zooming in and...*yes*! The covers of the silos have been rolled away and I think we will momentarily see—

—Thrax! One of our ever vigilant spotters has detected the presence of submarine launched ballistic missiles off the coast of one of the antagonists. Here, the picture's coming into view now.

—Excellent! Our calculations have this one about four minutes from detonation over...a major urban area!

—I think we can count on some real gore, folks.

—I must tell you, Blom, this will come as a bit of a treat after last week's rather slow-moving insurrection on Aullis Lost.

—That was definitely a disappointment. Oh! Oh! Observe, Thrax! Land-based missiles have been loosed. They have extremely low trajectories—obviously to avoid detection—but I think we can get a shot of them. Here they are, the little beauties...

—Really, really lovely aren't they? We can assume they're meant to decapitate civilian and military command and control facilities. Only 3.6 meters long, our statistician Xoxx tells me. Estimated time to impact: twelve minutes.

—We've got more activity, Thrax.

—Uh oh.

—They're unleashing the big boys now. Whoo!

—Blom, it's beautiful. So...*malevolent.* Folks, I hope this is coming in clear at home because from our position it looks simply majestic.

—Majestic is the word, Thrax. It's clear of the silo, in the initial phase of its flight. That flight will take it over the polar icecap and into the enemy's heartland. ETA about twenty-five minutes. Each of these babies is 21.5 meters long, 2.3 meters in diameter and they have an explosive yield on the average of...hang on to your hat—at least two hundred kilotons. They are relatively accurate for this type of weapon.

—Considering the technological backwardness of the planet.

—Yes, I was just about to add that postscript. Thrax, a number of the missiles have reached their boost phase so it shouldn't be long before the opposition's spy satellites pick them up—yes! That is exactly what has happened. *Their* silos are now opening, obviously in response to—

—Looks like they're hitting back with everything they have.

—This is going to be much, *much* better than we expected.

—Blom, there go more submarine launched missiles and we've got multiple bomber squadrons in flight. It's getting hard to keep track of them all.

—Each submarine carries in excess of two hundred warheads, enough to devastate a country on its own.

—More stats from Xoxx. Yeah! Those early missiles are moments from their targets and our preliminary calculations indicate we can expect heavy civilian casualties, not to mention lethal clouds of radiation that will contaminate great swathes of land for many years to come.

—That's the beauty of the things. THERE GOES ONE!

—Blom, let's zoom in on it. Beee-ooo—ti-ful.

—Sure is, Thrax. At the core of the explosion, the temperature is a stifling twenty-five million degrees. Now that kind of heat will convert the hardest elements to vapor as we can see in this shot here. Let's back that up and show it again in *excruciatingly* slow motion.

—Lovely.

—That building, the one directly in the center of the frame, will just evaporate...there, see it? Poof! Now we'll pull back a bit to give you some perspective...

—Kilometers of *nothing*.

—Exactly, Thrax. Everything has been blasted, burned and sucked up into that cloud, falling to earth over the next few days and weeks, perhaps even months. Highly radioactive, of course. Not that anyone down there will care.

—We've got some amazing footage of the blast wave, recorded moments ago by one of our superb camera operators.

—Look at it, Thrax! The speed and sheer *power*...everything in its path gathered up and swept away.

—And it appears we have a firestorm in the works! The incidental fires are definitely coalescing into one immense inferno that promises some exciting viewing.

—Folks, you're really getting your money's worth today

on "Mass Destruction, Devastation, Mayhem and Good, Clean Fun".

—Brought to you by Zoon's Ribbed Contraceptives.

—It's never too *Zoon* to be thinking about protection.

—Blom, we've got more bombers lumbering down runways on both sides, literally hundreds of planes in the air—

—Will we have time to get them on?

—I doubt it. Xoxx tells me they're rather slow-moving and will take hours to reach their intended targets. But we'll get clips of their run and highlight them on next week's show.

—As well as more good firestorm footage.

—No doubt.

—There goes another one, Thrax!

—And another!

—Someone should set this to music.

—Xoxx tells me that last one was—ready, Blom—*twenty megatons.*

—Whoo!

—We're talking about a crater a couple hundred meters deep and two and a half kilometers in diameter. What a monster!

—I'm just gonna sit back and enjoy the show.

—I'd like to remind you again that our sponsor is Zoon's Ribbed Contraceptives: accommodating all sizes, shapes and volumes. We'll be taking a station break in a few moments to give our affiliates a chance to identify themselves. Until then, we are pleased to be able to bring you the end of a civilization.

—Yeah, baby, go, go!

—This broadcast is copyrighted and any attempt to reproduce it, in whole or in part, is strictly prohibited. We will return in a moment...

## Man Disassembling

He pushes through the door of his apartment, then shuts it against the world. Bypassing the kitchen, he goes into the living room, where he lowers himself into a chair, sighing as he slips into its warm, pillowy embrace. Slowly, his sluggish movements betraying his exhaustion, he bends down, pops the snaps on his ankles and removes his aching feet. Lies back in the chair, closes his eyes, willing himself into a state of enforced lethargy. His left shoulder twitches spasmodically, a reaction to the day's rigorous exertions. He reaches up, unlatches the shoulder from its socket, lets the arm drop to the floor. He then divests himself of his legs, checking the hinged knees for signs of wear and tear before settling back in the chair. But then he feels a thrill of pain in his lower spine so he reaches back, depresses two switches and squirms out of his pelvic cavity. His head is throbbing, so with one practiced tug that goes too. But the respite is short-lived because then the phone rings—so he has to use his remaining arm to stick his head back on and reach for the receiver. Charlotte, it's always Charlotte, asking to see him, pleading with him, threatening him, *wailing* at him until finally he gets sick of listening to her and hangs up. In the time it takes her to re-dial, he peels off his ears and plucks out his tongue.

## "Arrival"

"Endean?" The voice was harried, fretful, immediately recognizable. He regretted answering the phone. "Have you read it? Has the courier delivered it yet?"

"Yes, it was dropped off about...forty-five minutes ago."

"What do you think of it?"

"I still have..." flipping to the end, "three more pages to read."

"You must have some impressions at least."

"It's very good."

"*Good*?" The voice parroted. "What has *that* got to do with anything? It's what it *says* that matters."

"Let's not jump to conclusions, Dennis."

"I'm not jumping to anything," his counterpart growled. "The story *reeks* of Intervention. My God, are you blind? Can't you see—"

"I'm not ready to go that far," he stated flatly.

"Well, *I* am."

"No," he said. "I'm not convinced. The evidence is not persuasive."

A pause.

"I intend to discuss this with the others."

"Fine." He retrieved the typescript. "Thank you for calling."

"Endean?" He waited. "For all of our sakes, I hope you're right."

He replaced the receiver, found the spot where he'd left off.

As he read the concluding paragraphs, he felt some of his certainty evaporate away; part of him couldn't help wondering if Dennis Groh's fears weren't justified after all:

> *He sensed that the atmosphere in the chamber was changing. At first the changes registered only peripherally, a furtive interplay of light and shadow. Then, as he looked on, spellbound, a translucent sheen settled over every visible object; even the walls and floor were affected and the ceiling,*

*if his eyes could be believed, was edging higher and higher.*

*In the center of the room, the coalescence had begun, a sudden flaring of silver-white light. Bergen retreated from the hot glare, shielding his face with his arms. The coruscating silver light blistered his hands, laid siege to the delicate tissues of his eyes. His pupils and retinas seared, he groped blindly about the room only to encounter something resembling tentacles, lunatic limbs studded with eyes. He shrieked as he was entwined and subdued by the powerful appendages, swiftly propelled into the slavering maw of the ageless fiend, devoured in three snapping bites.*

*It was not the repast it had contemplated throughout its prolonged exile but the entity was comforted by information relayed by its delicate sensory apparatus. There were other tasty morsels to be had...*

*...just beyond that puny door.*

Endean arranged and straightened the pages, snagged

them with a paper clip. He lay back against the cushions, a tired, old man who had yet to find the peace of mind most people his age assumed naturally, like an extra blanket against the cold.

His fingers brushed the pages.

Is it, he wondered, a clever, imaginative story...or something else, something more sinister?

An *invitation*, perhaps?

A querulous conscience subjected him to a stern cross-examination of his motives and moral character, the principles that guided and defined him. Did he really believe in what he was doing any more? Should he be in a position of responsibility if he was having such profound doubts?

In time he was able to rouse himself, reached over and picked up a pad and pen.

> "Suggest that you pass on this story. Do not give the author the benefit of a personal response. To be treated as just another offering from the 'slush pile'.
>
> I would like to take this opportunity to thank you, once again, for your continuing

cooperation. My colleagues and I are very much in your debt."

He signed the note, attached it to the story and set it aside.

Turning off the lights, he prepared himself for bed. Realizing all the while that there would be no sleep that night, not while the question, the one that kept repeating itself over and over like an annoying mantra, remained unanswered.

Too far or not far enough?

Too far or not far enough?

Too far or...

"Hello? Hello? Yeah, I'm still holding. Jesus Christ, lady, this is long distance, y'know. Hello? Ah, *shit*!" James Forbister knocked back some more scotch, paced back and forth, back and forth, as far as the cord would allow. "Yeah, I'm still here. Yes, I realize that but could he—" He gave up. "Right, well, tell him to phone me as soon as he's through." He hung up, went into the kitchen and replenished his glass. Then he read the letter again. In fifty words or less, it told him he could take his collection of short stories and stuff them in his arse. A cover note from his agent, Martin Schiller, urged him to "look on the bright side, at least a big-time editor give you serious consideration. This is the highest up  the food chain you've ever been. Once you crack that novel—" *hint, hint*, "we'll really be rolling. The door is open, now all we have to do is walk through it".

Marty, putting his usual hopeful spin on things.

The phone!

He pounded into the living room, grabbed it before the second ring.

"Hello, Jim." Schiller's voice sounded exactly like an agent's voice should:  smooth and ingratiating.

"Marty, what the hell happened? I thought it was a done deal."

"I was surprised too. At the last minute they got cold feet. The market for short story collections is diddly-squat right now. The last two they did tanked, big time. It's simple economics."

"But the stories were connected. It's like a—an episodic novel—"

"But it *isn't* a novel. Not in their eyes. And that's what they're after, that's what you should be shooting for, I keep telling you that. You come up with something, even if it's an outline, I'll get you a sweet advance." It was an old refrain and they both knew it by heart.

"I just don't think that way. These pieces of mine, they're more like flashes. It's hard to explain. They don't seem to sustain themselves beyond a few thousand words."

"We *need* a novel."

"But why? Let's keep trying to sell the stories. You've had some luck, why not try and build—"

"Jim, let's be honest here." Marty's voice took on an uncharacteristically harsh tone. "Most of your fiction is going to the small presses or genre magazines. That's not gonna get you the groundswell you need. You need exposure and you need a profile. And that means a novel. You can't live on that option money forever. That was a lucky break but it's not going to be a regular occurrence."

"Last I heard it's currently in 'hiatus'. That's one movie that's never gonna be made."

"In that case, you'd better make their little stipend last as long as you can."

"Okay, okay. But I still say those stories are good and—and people would read them if they were given the chance. I think if I keep building up a reputation—"

"A reputation don't buy you a cup of coffee in this town. Look kid," Marty, pouring on the charm again, "I gotta run. Things to do, people to see and all that. I'll keep putting in a good word for you."

"Okay." There wasn't much more to say. "Uh, Marty, you're going to keep flogging the collection, right? You won't give up on it? Emily Weeks is at HarperCollins now, isn't she? She likes my stuff—"

"I'll see she gets it." Marty Schiller promised. "I've got a couple of other places in mind too." A beat. "Listen, um, Jim, I don't want you getting your hopes up with this one. I just don't see it happening. This collection doesn't have a lot of, uh, commercial appeal. I know we've talked about this before…"

"Yeah, yeah," the beleaguered writer acknowledged.

"Your stories are too dark. Dark is okay sometimes but with you it's unrelenting. You gotta give people hope. And these latest stories, that *fantasy* stuff you sent me—what the heck am I supposed to do with it? They might be fine as far as these things go but, really, isn't it a bit *beneath* you? Bogeymen and secret societies..."

"But it's all part of a grand, encompassing mythology I'm developing. It keeps growing and becoming more complex, this whole cosmology—"

"I'd save that stuff for the trunk," his agent advised. "It's too kooky. Concentrate on the novel. Get that out of the way first."

"Yeah." Glumly. "I'll be talking to you, I guess."

"Back to the grind. Ta, Jim."

He drank the rest of the liquor in his glass then thought *what the hell* and went to get some more.

By the time he made it over to the desk he was feeling no pain. Numb. The keyboard blurred-focused-blurred. He blinked lazily.

Gotta cut down on the booze...start getting high on life...some day...

He sought the proper posture, cracked his knuckles, crabbed his fingers, faced the monitor, waited—

*waited*

It started, as always, with a whisper, almost inaudible, right at the edge of awareness. It seemed to originate from a point a few inches above and behind his head. Volume controls were adjusted, there was some fine-tuning and soon he was picking up words, sentences, paragraphs, the reception improving with each page.

Four thousand, two hundred and ninety-eight words later, the story was told and his muse departed without so much as a sprinkle of fairy dust.

*The End*, James Forbister typed.

And then passed out on his mousepad.


The story kept getting bounced. Marty Schiller sincerely tried but no one he approached expressed any enthusiasm for "Evocation". Maybe it was too retro. "If any of those pulps were still around," Schiller mused, "they might go for it. At, like, a penny a word."

"Doesn't *Playboy* take dark fantasy? They've printed Barker and King, haven't they?"

"Listen, Jim, forget *Playboy*, forget *Atlantic Monthly*.

You wanna play in the big leagues, you gotta choose serious subject matter. Nobody's interested in this crazy shit. You want to start selling more stories? Okay, here's my advice: throw away the fuckin' thesaurus. All this 'stygian' and 'opalescent' and 'eldritch' shit. It's too descriptive and wordy. People don't want that. They want a fast read, snappy dialogue. Think Elmore Leonard, not lost gods or whatever. Until then, forget *Playboy*. It's not gonna happen."

In the end, *Father Goose* took "Evocation". It was a digest-sized magazine out of Maryland devoted to fables and fairy tales from around the world. They were in the process of putting together a special Lovecraft issue. They paid him seventy-five dollars. Less Marty's fifteen per cent...

James Forbister heard the sound of one hand clapping. And hated it.

He threw himself into work. And drinking. Often at the same time. His prose took on increasingly hallucinatory qualities. Marty didn't think any of it was saleable. He kept bugging him about the fucking novel.

The lies came easily: *no problem, coming along fine. Have something for you by the fall...*he wasn't sure Marty believed him. He wasn't sure he cared.

During the summer he wrote a story called "Arrival" that was so good it blew his mind. Okay, it was weird, *really* weird and there were whole sections he couldn't remember writing. What the hell, lots of authors wrote blind drunk. There was something about it, it seemed to access older, darker parts of his mind. It was unquestionably powerful and evocative work, a tale that seemed, at least to his eyes, original and well told.

He left a message with Marty Schiller, babbling on and on about "Arrival", giddy with excitement. At that point he hadn't slept for ninety-two hours, so he could be forgiven for sounding somewhat frazzled.

Marty would understand, once he read the story.

"Arrival" caused another late night phone call and heated debate.

"The portents, Endean, you can hardly deny them. Look around you. The world is literally going to hell."

"I read the news."

"Sure you do. But you refuse to accept the evidence of outside machinations. I have files and files of material that tell of brutal and obscene acts committed by supposedly civilized, rational individuals. The power of our ancient enemy is growing with each passing day."

"I see no method to this madness," Endean demurred. "You see design, I see random acts of savagery. Your reasoning has failed to sway me...yet again."

The phone sputted and cracked. Then: "We'll see what happens at the next Gathering."

"I think you overestimate your powers of persuasion, Dennis. The Committee voted against you last time—"

"Not by much, my friend."

"Nevertheless, you must abide by the terms of the Pact. You cannot act independently against James Forbister."

"You needn't bring up the Pact. I assure you I know every word of it by heart."

"And you'll use every pretext to go after him, won't you?" Endean challenged.

"It is our sworn duty to uphold the integrity of this dimension. We cannot allow Incorporeality to—"

The dogmatic fervor of his colleague wore Endean down. He dearly wanted to say something pithy but ended up muttering: "He's a human being. Not a toy to be played with. He's a man of talent, of vision. He could do a lot of good for this world."

The caller dismissed his remarks brusquely. "We nearly waited too long before."

Yes, he'd been expecting Dennis to raise that point sooner or later. The close calls. The zealots liked to invoke writers and artists the Committee had dealt with in the past, names derived from a roll call of infamy. It never failed to cause a stir at Gatherings. These perverse talents had allied themselves, wittingly or not, with the forces of chaos and despair—their creative endeavors, so the reasoning went, serving to nudge a slumbering evil toward wakefulness. The Committee had dealt with them, all of them, sometimes very harshly. A number were made to suffer a great deal during their brief, inglorious careers. Endean felt nothing but pity for them.

For instance...take the treatment accorded a certain reclusive resident of Providence, Rhode Island, one Howard Phillips Lovecraft.

Lovecraft's fertile imagination took him where no one

had dared go before and as a result he was singled out for special attention. He became the object of a concerted campaign waged by agents affiliated with the Committee. He proved to be astonishingly resilient, refusing to be dissuaded from writing of the Old Ones and their designs on the planet they had once ruled as gods. He endured penury and anonymity and indignity, meanwhile toiling ceaselessly at his craft. Thanks to the Committee, Lovecraft died without ever receiving his just due, the acclaim he so richly deserved...that would not come until many years later.

The man speaking had a similar fate in store for Jim Forbister, of that Endean was certain. Moments later there was confirmation. "He must be stopped. *Now*. At the next Gathering I will propose a series of steps that should convince our friend to abandon his chosen vocation. Perhaps he'll take up acting, like that Welshman. What was his name again?"

"Machen."

"That's the one." Dennis Groh cleared his throat. "Endean, surely you realize that if our enemy manages to gain even a foothold—"

"Yes, I've heard the legends," he replied. It was a serious

slip and Groh quickly pounced on it.

"*Legends?* That sounds like blasphemy to me."

"Don't be a fool," Endean barked.

"I think you should know that I've been recording this conversation."

"Damn you, Dennis—"

The phone hummed spitefully in his hand.


"Marty?"

"Yes, Jim." Schiller's voice sounded flat, disinterested.

"Um, I was wondering what you thought of the story I sent you. You should've gotten it last week."

One of those awkward pauses. "Help me out with this one, will you, kiddo," Schiller coaxed.

"Haven't you read it yet?"

"I remember getting it but I've been busy and--"

"*Jeezus.* I guess I assumed that when my agent gets my stuff, it's his job to—"

"Wait, wait, I'm finding it." He could hear Schiller opening drawers, rustling papers…a dyspeptic belch and the agent was back. "'The Arrival', right?"

"Just 'Arrival'."

"Yeah, but, see this is what I was talking about. Lenore read it and she says it's more of that fantasy crap. This type of thing isn't doing your career any favors and, like I've already told you, Jimbo, it's a road to nowhere."

"But have *you* read it?"

"I skimmed it or whatever—"

"*Skimmed* it? Holy shit. I don't believe it. You *skimmed* it?" He almost ate the telephone.

"I told you, it isn't my type of thing. And it's not exactly easy on the eyes. Long paragraphs and—"

"You don't read my work, you don't return my calls. It's like you've given up on me. What's changed? Why—why are you fucking with me?"

"—hold on a minute—"

But he wouldn't. He couldn't. "You don't give a shit about me! You don't give a shit about my words, my mind—"

"—hanging up, call me when you get a grip on yourself."

He flung the telephone away. After that he killed the rest of the scotch. It died a glorious death. He flopped into his chair, swiveled it around until he faced his bookshelves.

Tomes by authors like Matheson, Beaumont, Bradbury, Calvino and Dick mocked him like Inquisitors: *You're nothing! Look at us! You don't belong up here! You never will...*

No, he thought, I suppose you're right. I'm Jim Forbister. A legend in my own mind.

He pounded his fists on his knees, suffused with rage.

Why can't I get a break, just one fucking break? Is it too much to ask?

Never mind. None of this shit mattered. He wasn't going to let them beat him. He'd keep on trying, keep hammering his head against the wall. Nothing was going to stop him until he broke through and saw for himself what was on the other side...

The show of bravado lasted until he sat down at the keyboard. He experienced the same surge of panic he always did when he started a new story. Would this be the day he heard the gurgle as the last reserves of his creativity and inspiration drained away?

No.

Listen, his Muse said, I have something to tell you. A

deep, dark secret. Ready?

Halfway through the story he shuddered; the imagery was so *gory*, the whole thing far more graphic and vicious than he expected. By the time he got to the last few lines he was shaking so hard he could barely control his hands.

When he finished, his keyboard seemed unnaturally hot. He wrote himself a quick *Post-It* note, a reminder to take in his aging computer, have them run a diagnostic, find out what the problem was...

The Gathering was a stormy one.

Endean's coalition rallied bravely but many on the Committee of the Seventy-One were clearly disturbed by Forbister's latest fictional offering.

"It carries the taint," one longtime Committee member was heard to remark.

"Almost certainly a work inspired by the enemy," another murmured.

A sense of foreboding gripped many of those present. These were evil times, populated by men and women who could look on unflinchingly as millions the world over perished or suffered needlessly, who could cheat and lie and steal and seduce and corrupt and despoil with the minimum of mental discomfiture.

Endean did not dispute any of this. He argued, however, that there was no tangible evidence to link Forbister or his writing to the present, admittedly rotten state of affairs in the world. That's when he heard the names again, whispered by those loyal to Groh.

Machen...Smith...Crowley...Chambers...Blake...Bosch...

And, of course: Lovecraft...Lovecraft...*Lovecraft*...

Endean knew he'd lost even before the grim-faced Chair announced the results of the secret ballot and put the matter in the hands of Dennis Groh's faction.

"It's too much," he told them. "You must show restraint. There's no need to destroy this man."

He received no reassurances. It was out of his hands.

James Forbister was at their mercy.

Nothing could save him now.


He was drunk again, laughing and singing, careening around his dark warren of an apartment, sloshing booze all over himself. Someone thumped on the ceiling.

"FUCK YOU!" He yelled.

God, what a *stink*. Well, he'd have to start cleaning up soon, he was nearly out of glasses. Har har har. On second thought, who gave a shit about how funky it smelled? No one had been by in...how long? The last person he talked to was his mother and he'd ended *that* conversation by calling her gutless and old and pathetic and hanging up on her. No more *Care* packages from home. Looking on the bright side, it meant he saved money on holiday and birthday cards.

Whup! Whup!

He grabbed his chair and hung on for dear life. The room tilted one way and then cunningly reversed direction; he planted both feet to compensate. Decided it might be a smart move to sit down. He did. Wheeled over to his work area, collected the story from on top of the printer. He touched his keyboard and, *yikes*, it was radiating heat. He used his mouse, shut everything off. Those fucking geeks at the repair place, telling him there was nothing wrong. *Okay, bright boys, then how come I got a machine so fucking hot I could fry an egg on it?* He unplugged the power bar from the wall, just to be on the safe side.

After weeks and weeks of *nothing*, of not being able to give away a three-line poem to a small press 'zine with a readership of six (including the publisher's parents), this sucker just *came* to him, fully formed. Uncanny? Oh, yeah. In more ways than one.

He wished he could call Marty Schiller to brag about it...except he had ripped the phone out of the wall during one of his drunken rages and still hadn't gotten someone over to fix it.

Instead he raised his glass, toasting his loyal Muse.

Here's to you, babe...


"ENDEAN!"

"Wha—oh, it's you, Dennis."

"He's done it this time, do you hear me?" Gasping with excitement. "I've just finished his latest story, delivered to one of our people an hour ago. Are you listening? He's defining the Intangible. Every word, every adjective, every modifier seeks to provide It with more substance. *It*. 'The worm of corruption, the worm that dieth not.'." The man was distraught, babbling. Endean's guts tightened and he could feel his heart speeding up. "—we too late? Answer me, Endean. *Are we too late?*"

"No!" But he was rattled, his thoughts resisting any imposition of order. "Have we—do you have his address?"

"I have it," Groh confirmed. "What are you—"

"Give it to me!"

His Muse was anxious to get to work. That was fine with him. That last story really fired him up, got the creative juices flowing.

He was receptive so the spell quickly overcame him, held him effortlessly. But this time it was different, *everything* was different. His consciousness was brushed aside, relegated to the role of mere spectator, his Muse taking over completely, bypassing his brain, possessing his fingers, compelling them to fly across the keyboard at a phenomenal speed. It was scary but *fan-fucking-tastic* to watch.

He zipped through the story, no stopping for corrections, no spell-checking, just *brrrrrup*! Like a fucking machine gun.

And what a tale it was, savage, bleak and blasphemous;

horror in its purest form, primal and awful and malign. His stomach bubbled up in his throat. He gagged. His eyes filled with tears but he couldn't look away, he had to know what happened next, bear witness to the outrages and atrocities committed against flesh and blood people who blew their last living breath in his face.

Please...please...tell me: where is hope?

Gone.

Love?

Forgotten.

Goodness?

Disbelieving laughter.

He couldn't hear Endean pounding on his door. The shouts and splintering wood. The keyboard was literally smoking, his fingertips sizzling when they touched the keys; he felt pain but it was miles away, only vaguely perceived.

His Muse wouldn't let him go. While he watched, helpless, a *thing* was born, words granting it gruesome features, leathery folds of skin, broad, powerful wings and a variety of grasping, tearing appendages.

He typed in a name, a jumble of consonants.

*Something happened.* The room changed. Not its physical properties, nothing you could empirically measure— no, the alteration registered in an ancient area of his brain, triggering alarms, raising gooseflesh.

As soon as the last period was in place, his Muse cut the strings, returning the borrowed body to its rightful owner. His wrists and forearms ached and most of his fingertips sported livid blisters. Cradling his throbbing hands, he leaned closer so he could read the last words he'd typed—

*It burst out of the screen*, fastening on to him, rending and tearing at his body with a thousand sharp teeth...


The cold and the stench told Endean all he needed to know. His eyes sought out and found the portal—a shattered monitor, the hole still smoking and crackling, leaking circuitry and leaded glass.

Chunks of glistening flesh and charred clothing were scattered in the vicinity, red and purple fragments cooling on the desk and carpet. Unidentified human remains. Chewed and partially digested.

Endean's knees snapped and popped as he knelt. He

began to pray fervently, desperately, but already he sensed that the atmosphere in the chamber was changing. At first the changes registered only peripherally, a furtive interplay of light and shadow. Then, as he looked on, spellbound, a translucent sheen settled over every visible object; even the walls and floor were affected and the ceiling, if his eyes could be believed, was edging higher and higher.

In the center of the room, the coalescence had begun...

## Final Showing

Stan tried to look cool, did his best to blend in with the bored pedestrians crowding the Saturday night sidewalks. He was too hyper, the adrenaline coursing through him kept him on edge, fearful and paranoid, practically jumping out of his skin. He stood out like a sore thumb—he needed to find some place where he could regroup and get his shit together.

So: the movie theater.

A porno movie theater with a cracked, flickering marquee, *SKIN FLIX All Day All Night Even Christmus*. There were missing bulbs, the tang of fresh piss and some old moll of a ticket taker preserved in a plastic bubble by the front door. Maintained in her own natural habitat, floating in an airtight beaker of toxic cigarette smoke.

He paid for a ticket with the first bill off the roll. Got his change and hurried inside.

The shakes hit him bad when he was paying for a drink. As he reached for the cup it was like his hand spasmed or something, spilling the cold beverage all over the counter. Young bitch in charge wasn't impressed as she swabbed up the mess. Even made him pay for another drink.

As soon as he stepped through the curtain into the seating area, he felt a thousand times better. *This is great,* he enthused as he walked down the aisle, taking a seat about six rows from the front, prime viewing position. *I'll sit in here with these congenital losers and fuckups until I mellow out and then be on my merry way. Celebrating the fruits of my labor.*

The bills crackled in his pocket, their presence a tactile reminder of the events of the past ten or fifteen minutes. He felt the bundle. How much? Two hundred? Three hundred, if he was lucky. Maybe enough to put things right for awhile but time was running out, his options disappearing one by one. It wasn't looking good. He was down to this now, a bottom-feeder.

He reached into the other pocket, touched the gun. His fingers came away stippled with blood and trailing spidery wisps of hair. He wiped his hands on his jeans, wiped and wiped until he'd gotten it all off.

*Stupid old fuck.*

He was shaking again. *Shouldn't—shouldn't of reached under the counter like that. I coulda shot him, blown him away. Would've served him right. Jesus, he went down like a ton of bricks. And the blood...*he rubbed his fingers on his pants again. *I gotta be crazy pulling this shit. It ain't my style and it ain't solving anything.*

It was like he was on one of those treadmill things, running as fast as he could but getting nowhere. Sooner or later he was going to get caught and if he wasn't killed, they'd lock him up with people who would be happy to finish the job for them.

He stretched in his seat; his bones creaked like rusty hinges. God, he was tight. Tight as a wound spring. Tight as Tinkerbell's twat. He grinned. Tight as a miser's purse. Tighter 'n a Jew's ass. Tight as a—

He started giggling.

"Shaddap," someone snapped from the near dark.

The place smelled bad, a potent combination of sweat,

piss and other bodily secretions he didn't care to think about. The immorality plays depicted in the grainy, amateurish films had had a corrosive effect on the once-lavish interior. The screen was old, patched, threadbare. The walls were peeling, water-damaged, the floor should have been stickered by the EPA and the seats, well, the less said of their appearance and condition, the better.

The patrons hadn't been spared either. They had been worn down, winnowed away by their prolonged exposure to smut. Stan had seen their faces as he came in, features split and pockmarked by ten lifetimes of travails, cross-hatched by bitterness and grief and despair. Most of them sat alone, avoiding human contact, finding solace in personal perversions and delusions. This was a place of refuge for those who had experienced more than their fair share of suffering while cruising the dirty boulevards in pursuit of broken down dreams.

He looked up at the screen in time to be menaced by a closeup view of a guy getting head. He was practically being *devoured* by this woman who, like a snake, seemed capable of dislocating her jaw to accommodate larger pieces of meat.

Stan stirred restlessly in his seat. He'd seen plenty of porno stuff in his time—hell, who hasn't—but it still made him sort of uncomfortable to be sitting there, watching. He wasn't queer or anything, it was just that when they showed everything up close and personal it made sex look, well, *obscene.*

To Stan, sex had always been a pleasant, if over-rated experience. He thought he handled himself pretty well, not a cocksman maybe but no Quick Draw McGraw either. He couldn't remember sex ever looking like *that.* That wasn't the way two normal human beings did it. They resembled a couple of wild animals up there, sucking and slurping away at each other. Was this supposed to turn you on? It was the equivalent of watching two dogs go at it in the street. He decided to ignore the movie—*uh uh yeah, baby, c'mon*—and count the money instead.

Stan pulled the roll from his pocket, admiring its heft; he arranged the bills and began the tally, sometimes finding it hard to read denominations because of the poor illumination.

Meanwhile things were definitely heating up onscreen.

—five, ten, twenty, thirty—

"—*uh huh, uh huh, that's it, baby, that's it, ohhhh, you got it*—"

—fifty, fifty-five—

"—*feels so good, oh, like I'm gonna melt all over you*—"

—sixty, sixty-five...was that a ten or a five?

He gathered up the money, started again, doing his best to blot out the grunting, thudding cacophony. He was concentrating so hard on getting the count right—

"Hey, buddy..."

—that he had reached the two hundred mark before he realized—

"Hey, I'm talking to you..."

—something had gone wrong—

"You hear me, boy?"

—all wrong—

"I SAID 'WHAT THE FUCK DO YOU THINK YOU'RE DOIN?'"

—tragically and irrevocably wrong.

His hand hovered in the air, holding the next bill, a twenty.

"Low-life, pistol-whipping, motherfucking goon, that's

what you are."

Stan slowly raised his eyes.

The couple had changed positions. The man was pumping her from behind while staring directly at the camera. Directly at *Stan.*

"That's right, boy. Look *waaaay* up here. That's it. Now you got it."

Stan's mouth filled with sand.

"You killed that old man," the porn star, listed in the credits as Long John Quayle, told him. "Cracked his skull like a fucking egg. That makes you a murderer. And there ain't nothin' lower than that." And all the while he was, like, banging away on the woman, never missing a stroke. She didn't seem to notice the rather odd turn the plot had just taken—or didn't care.

Stan sensed movement behind him. He twisted around but his fellow viewers gave no indication of having stirred. Except they were all two or three seats closer to him. He blinked and they seemed closer still.

He turned back to the screen. Telling himself *easy there, guy, don't go losing it on me.*

He took a deep breath and held it. Then slowly let it out. That was better.

*Okay, listen up:*

*This is what's commonly referred to as a freakout and the best thing to do is just let it go, ride it out. What it is is that you're worried about the old guy in the liquor store. That's it, you're worried and you're scared shitless because you ain't no master criminal and you ain't hard. You're just desperate. And it's fucking with your head. So you gotta get this under control, suck it up and stay frosty and everything will be all right.*

The money looked dirty and crumpled and sodden. It felt like he was holding somebody's garbage. He thrust it back into his pocket.

"Mister...Mister?" An ugly little man with a twisted lip was tapping him on the arm. "I saw ya drop dis on the way in. Here y'are..."

And he was automatically accepting a small pebble, a black, cinder-like nugget that smelled like steaming fresh dogshit. Stan gave an exclamation of disgust and cast it away. "That was your soul," the man told him, "your rotten, evil soul."

"Get the fuck out of my face," Stan rasped.

"Your soul," he repeated, shambling away.

Cruel, derisive laughter from overhead.

And Stan thought, right, fuck this noise, ready or not, I'm outta here.

The amplified voice of Long John Quayle resounded again. "Fucker thinks he's just gonna get up and *leave*." The woman was on top of him now, thrusting her hips half-heartedly while mouthing the usual stock entreaties. His head was lolling over the side of the bed and he was looking—there was no use denying it—at Stan and no one else. "Forget it, killer. You're not going anywhere."

Stan pushed up from his seat, rising—and then he was falling back, windmilling his arms in a vain attempt to stay upright, nearly breaking his back across an armrest.

WHAT THE FUCK?

His feet wouldn't move. He tried tugging on his legs but his running shoes were secured to the floor by the sticky residue of spilled drinks (and who knows what else) from time immemorial. There was no give to the stuff; he was stuck fast.

"Take him," the porn star instructed them, pulling the woman down to him. "He's not one of us. Send him to Hell, where he belongs."

As Stan bent and began to fumble with his laces, he could hear them coming.

He sat up and saw they were edging along his row and those parallel to it, closing the distance. Their glazed, fixed expressions were unnerving. Stan got one shoe off but then his sock got embedded in the resistant goo. He was working on the other sneaker when the first one reached him, seizing his hair and jerking Stan's head back while groping for his balls with the other hand.

Stan fucking lost it. He grabbed a fistful of the guy's shirt and pulled him partially over the seat. Punched him in the face, three good, hard shots that cracked his knuckles. But the freak seemed unfazed, hanging on to Stan, grinning a bloody, gap-toothed grin.

The others moved in, snatching at Stan's flailing fists. He screamed for help, hoping someone would hear and call the cops. He clawed for the gun but the pocket was empty—must have fallen out. When he bent to retrieve it from the floor he found it stuck fast and then they were on top of him, forcing him down. His hands went out instinctively and were immersed in the goo. Their combined strength pressed his face into the sticky mess, rendering him helpless.

Then they killed him. With their fists and feet and their fingernails and their teeth.

When they were finished, when his battered body refused to expel another ragged breath, they left him, returned to their seats. Few paid any mind to the hissing, spitting sound the goo made as it went to work on Stan's corpse, reducing it to a brown, viscous puddle. They were once again engrossed in the movie.

The onscreen couple were indulging in some post-coital banter while they enjoyed a cigarette.

"Was it good for you, baby?" Long John Quayle, returning to the script, inquired of Suzie Wett.

The camera framed her face. She was plain but not homely. From the neck down maybe a seven out of ten. "Honey," she purred, "I'll tell you one thing: you sure know how to treat a lady."

They'd heard the joke hundreds of times by now. Maybe

it was force of habit. Or something instinctive. It was hard to know.

But for some reason that line always got a big laugh.

*Monologue*

Jesus H. Christ, I've never seen it stacked up like this before. If Ryerson hadn't raked my ass over the coals for my impertinence, laziness and overall bad-ass motherfucking attitude, I'd be home right now, sucking back an ice cold Coors. Instead here I am, stuck in the worst snarl-up in the history of the world and I've got less than a quarter tank of gas and I'm about *this* close to blowing my top. I could probably get out and crawl on my belly faster than this. Yeah, then along comes this little chink on a motorcycle, zipping in and out of traffic, making the rest of us round-eyed bastards in our gas-guzzling, air conditioned coffins look like a bunch of fucking idiots. We bombed you, you little yellow fucker, bombed you into submission. And we could do it again if we wanted to.

I don't believe this. They're playing the worst shit on the

radio. Maybe I can find some jazz. Disco...disco...disco. Techno crap. All these stations sound the same. There, baby: the sounds of silence.

Moving again. Maybe five feet that time.

This is absolutely incredible. I mean, we're supposed to be this modern society, the world is chockfull of technological marvels and every day at four o'clock exactly everything just breaks down. And here we are: primitive man.

Whoa! What are you doing? You can't cut in! Fuck! Hey, cocksucker! You nearly nailed my bumper there, buddy. Fucking guy cut in like he was the king of fucking Siam. Look at him. The square-headed, bristle-haired Nazi fascist prick. You'd better watch your mirror. I'm here. Yeah, gonna get nice and close. You just sit there and sweat while I shove my four thousand pound cock up your ass.

Stopping again.

When's the next turn off? Anything comes up and I'll try to sneak across and—yeah, right, I do that and someone's liable to blow my head off. It's happened before.

OH, COME ON!

You'd think there'd be some cops around, directing

traffic or something. Our city's finest are probably sitting on their fat arses dunking doughnuts and lying about the last time they got laid.

Hey, wake up, buddy, we're moving! Up yours. I'm honking 'cause you ain't moving, bub.

Your mother, asshole.

Jesus, call Wiesenthal, I found Mengele at last.

Hey, hey, lady, watch what—FUCK!

You stupid, blind, blundering, titless twat!

God, give me the strength to deal with these—yeah, yeah, hi yourself. Doesn't look so bad? Lady, are you nuts? Where's your white cane? That little ding is gonna set me back—*my* insurance? Like this was *my* fault? Listen to these people honking. Give us a break here! There's been an accident! Lady, I got a deductible that'll cost me more than what you paid for that hunk of shit you're driving. Will you listen to them? And they won't let up. All right, already! Just...let's forget it, okay? Get back in your car and *go*. And I hope you roll on the way home and you're crippled for life and your kids have to go into hock to pay your medical bills.

We're moving again, praise the Lord.

At least Herr Shithead is gone. What's this? Kansas plates. Okies. Fucking redneck hayseeds. C'mon, folks, this ain't Niagara Falls.

Hmmm...getting right down to "E". That's just great. And when the tank runs dry I'm gonna keep the air conditioning and radio going until the battery dies and then I'm just gonna sit here in the middle of the freeway, a monument to the WILLFUL FUCKING IGNORANCE OF MAN.

God, I'm telling you this right now: if I don't get a break pretty soon I'm gonna wig out and hurt one of your fine creations. Like Ryerson. I'd love to do that scrawny, wrinkled little prick in. And Autry. I know that scumbag has been ratting on me to the old man. I'd love to get my thumbs on his eyeballs and shove them back into his brain.

Ten feet that time. I'm flat out fucking enjoying myself here. I haven't had this much fun since my last divorce.

Let's try Mr. Radio again. Traffic info. Multi-car pileup. Yeah. let's hear about it.

Yeah, yeah, I knew it. Half the people driving should never have been given a license in the first place. Jeez, I wonder how bad it is. Hope I get there before they have everything cleaned up.

Looks like I'll be here awhile. Keep it in neutral, save gas. I'll never make it at this rate. No way. Why didn't I get gas this morning? Answer: because I didn't want to be late knowing Ryerson has some kind of bug up his ass. That prick fucked up my whole day.

I'd like to wreck his life. Rape his ugly wife and make him watch. About halfway through she'd probably start enjoying herself and that would *really* drive him batshit. Aw, who am I trying to kid? I could never fuck that old hag. My dick would never forgive me.

I can't take much more of this shit! I really fucking can't! If all you assholes weren't such shitty drivers we wouldn't have this problem. I was driving when most of you were still sucking your mothers' tits.

C'mon, pal, get moving. What's the hold up?

Let's go!

What?

WHAT?

Over-heated? Over-fucking-heated? Are you kidding me?

You stupid, slab-headed ignoramus! Why bring a lemon

like that on the freeway in the first place? You lousy stinking piece of shit—

Lay off those horns! It's not me, it's *him*.

Hey, I'm not just gonna sit here waiting for you. No way, buddy. Get it off the road, will ya—

I SAID 'PUSH IT OFF TO THE SIDE'. You stupid asshole.

I got plans, mister, appointments.

Huh?

JUST PUSH IT OFF TO THE SIDE—

Will you lay off those horns?

Mister, get in your car and I'll use mine to push you. You just steer. Yeah, yeah, don't worry about it. I've done this before.

Get your ass in gear, you dumb Polack.

Whoops! SHIT! That's his tail light. Fuck, he looks pissed—

Sorry about that, pal, it kind of jumped ahead on me.

Hey, HEY, MISTER, YOU DON'T HAVE TO—

DON'T KICK MY CAR, DON'T—

—you fuck, oh, you lousy fuck—

YOU'RE DEAD, MISTER, YOU HEAR ME?

YOU DENTED MY CAR AND YOU'RE FUCKING DEAD!

## The Hibakusha *
### for Kinuko Laskey

She was getting desperate.

Despite her heart-rending pleas, the doctor remained unmoved. "No, absolutely *not*, Mrs. Morrow. We simply can't accommodate any more patients, especially those who require that level of care."

"But this is a *hospital*. You're supposed to take care of the sick—or have you forgotten your Hippocratic Oath?"

"I'm quite conversant with the oath, ma'am, but circumstances have changed and I'm afraid it can't be taken quite so literally any more." The doctor, whose name was Phelps or Phillips, she couldn't remember which, was clearly growing impatient with her.

---

* *hi-bok´-sha* "This word was newly coined after the bombing (of Hiroshima and Nagasaki). It meant 'explosion affected person(s)' or 'the people who received the bomb'." From *Day One: Before Hiroshima and After* by Peter Wyden

"He's dying and you know it. You can't just let him—"

"Mrs. Morrow." His gaze was unrelenting. "I am aware of your husband's delicate condition. And I know how hard it must be for you..." His voice trailed off and she watched as he rubbed his red-rimmed, dolorous eyes. For not the first time she found herself pitying him, wondering how he managed to maintain a semblance of civility while engaged in the insurmountable task of tending to all the people, so many sick, dying people that the hospital had burst its seams; patients spilled out of its wards into its corridors, through the front doors and onto the grounds of the building. "I've seen many similar cases," he continued. "Yes, he needs special attention and treatment but so does everyone else in here. We're barely functioning as it is—our resources are nonexistent, our staff pushed to the very limits of endurance."

"So you're just going to write him off."

"Mrs. Morrow, take a look at this please." The doctor pulled up one sleeve of his crusty smock, revealing a series of purple blotches originating just above his wrist, spotting his forearm all the way up past his elbow. "I'd say it's going to be a week, maybe two, before I have to write myself off."

"A-at least let me have some pills, something to—"

"As I said, our supplies *are* limited. However, I think I can let you have some vitamins, perhaps some penicillin tablets—"

Kay regarded him with shock. "That's *it*? That's all you can give me?" The doctor shrugged. "You know, I've heard that you guys have access to lots of drugs. Some say you're holding out, maybe saving them for people willing to *pay*."

"Absolute nonsense!" He appeared genuinely affronted by the notion. "It's true that there were some drugs stockpiled before the war—morphine, for instance—but those reserves were quickly gobbled up. And those few labs that made it through everything relatively intact aren't coming *close* to meeting the demand. Pharmaceuticals will be in short supply for a long time to come, take my word for it." He scribbled something on a pad, tore it off, handed the slip to her. "Give this to Captain Rutherford upstairs. He's in charge of the detail guarding our stores. He'll draw your allotment for you."

Kay took the ineffectual piece of paper from him.

He wanted to say something as she turned away, apologize for his demeanor, perhaps express more words of commiseration.

He closed his mouth. That wasn't what she needed right now. She'd come to him expecting help. Instead, he'd robbed her of her last hope. He could see it, tell from the look on her face. She knew it was over. She'd already started to grieve...

Kay leaned against a pillar outside the hospital.

What was she going to do? The drugs were nearly gone. The next time she saw the doctor he might not give her anything. Like he said, he had worries of his own. She wondered if he'd be so stingy when it was *his* ass that was on the line.

"Didn't get anything, did you?"

The sallow-faced, perspiring man, attired in what had once been an expensive parka, shivered up at her from the bottom of the steps.

She ignored him.

"Told you there was nothing they could do for you, right?" he persisted.

"Leave me alone."

"What have you got?" She decided he was crazy. She

walked down the steps, bumped him aside with her shoulder as she passed. He grunted in anger and came after her. A hand tagged her shoulder, sought purchase. She balled her fist, got ready to let him have it—

"I can get you things." Speaking low, intimately, directly into her ear. "Dope. Pills. Uppers. Downers. Bottles of miracles, lady."

She turned around. "Where?"

"What have you got to trade for 'em?"

"Enough." The past few months had taught her to be discreet when bargaining.

"Are ya sure?" He was sneering and she didn't like that.

"I'm sure."

He nodded. "Okay, lady. If you're lyin' or trying any bullshit—"

"Don't threaten me."

"You meet me back here in one hour with as much as you can carry. You got that?"

"And you'll—"

He raised a finger. "One hour."

The trip home was accomplished with brisk, springy

strides.

Maybe just this once things would turn out all right. There had been so many disappointments and setbacks. *C'mon, God, get with the plan. Don't mean to complain, Big Guy, but you've been awfully conspicuous by your absence lately and I think maybe now might be a good time to pop in, shake some hands, kiss a few babies and, oh yeah, one more thing—*

She pushed open the door to the small apartment, old habits causing her to feel chagrined by the dirt and grime embedded in the carpet. Her footsteps raised small dust devils as she crossed the floor to the bedroom door. She inched it open.

"Kay...?"

"Hi, sweetheart." She knelt before him, wriggled in closer so he could see her better.

"Everything...is it..."

"Shhhh. Fine, baby, fine. Here." She raised his head, pressed the pills past his frayed lips. The accompanying water made him choke but the pills stayed down. "There. That wasn't so bad." She resettled him, straightened out the blankets.

"I...have to..."

By now she had become fluent at instantly deciphering his moment-to-moment needs. "Don't feel bad, just go ahead. Use the diaper and I'll wash you up afterwards."

As she looked on he endured a terrible coughing fit. *Stop it*, she silently implored. *Because right now you've got about three white blood cells in your whole body and if you catch so much as a cold...*she couldn't finish the thought.

The fit subsided.

"Better?" He nodded. "Want to know what I did today?" Another, almost imperceptible nod. "Well, after a *very* successful trip to the hospital, I stopped by the market and managed to swap for a drumstick. Don't ask me what we had to give up for it, it'll only depress you." When she checked for his reaction she saw that his eyes were shut. He seemed very still. She leaned over, close enough to feel him exhale onto her cheek. Just asleep then.

This time.

She stood, observing him as he slept, trying to imagine him as he used to be. Splicing together images and scenes from the past, assembling crudely edited recollections of her strong, awkward husband who had no taste whatsoever and called honey "bee shit" and loved staying up late to watch old Hammer horror movies.

That's how she wanted to remember him.

*I'm so sorry, my darling. I should have been in the city that day. I should have been with you. I heard about what you did, how you dug yourself out and tried to help as many people as you could. They called you a hero.*

Look at the hero now, weighing in at a strapping ninety pounds, as bald as a baby and just about as strong. He had to be changed constantly and dined on pablum and powdered milk, "the breakfast of champions" he called it, whenever he was cognizant enough to make the feeble joke.

She dreaded those occasional moments of lucidity, when he was awake and the fever down, the pain almost bearable. As she fluffed the pillows or helped him into a clean t-shirt she could feel his eyes on her and he would make the request again:

"Kay...let me die. Christ...Jesus...walk away and let me die."

She would stroke his forehead, wet his lips with a kiss, sit at his side until he dozed off. All the while wondering...*Could I? No, never. It won't come to that.* And then, plaintively: *please, God, don't let it come to that.*

After removing and disposing of his soiled things, Kay went into the kitchen to collect the goods she would barter. The cooler was in urgent need of another block of ice; the lettuce had blackened around the edges and some of the oranges were spongy when she gripped them. That meant another visit to Frank Finley's ice house. The old bastard wanted more and more each time she went. The virtue of controlling a monopoly.

She finished packing all she could afford to take, closed the hasps on the bag.

Kay debated going in to say good-bye to Sebastian but didn't like the finality the gesture implied. She settled for blowing him a kiss as she was leaving. Moments after the door shut behind her, he called out from the sick room, gasped her name as he thrashed about, in the scalding grip of a fever dream.

But she never heard him and so this time he bore his torments alone.

He found himself in a hypnagogic delirium: a vast, molten lake, white hot and limned with flames. There were people—old folks, children, babies—*burning alive*, dying in agony. And then feeling his own body engulfed in a bright, livid heat as he was submerged in the bubbling mire and the pain—oh, good Christ, the *pain*—

If only the pain would end...

He was right on time.

"Sure you got enough in there? You'd better or—"

"I told you to stop threatening me. Don't do it again."

"You're a tough one, ain't ya?" He sounded edgy. "Tough as nails, huh?"

"Just give the pills, will you?" She snapped.

"I don't have 'em."

She wanted to punch him, split his lips, knock his teeth down his lying throat. "You *said—*"

"I'm *taking* you to somebody who has 'em."

She got up close to him, right in his face. Butted his chest with a forefinger. "You don't get a damn thing until I get the pills, got it? And if you're thinking about taking me somewhere to cut me and leave me for the dogs, you'd better think again. I'll be watching you. And I'm not exactly helpless."

"You'll get what you're after, don't worry," he assured her. "And a lot more if you ain't careful," he added under his breath as he sidled away.


Kay was tired.

So much *walking*. He was taking her further and further into the shattered city, ignoring her queries, refusing to even acknowledge them. He never paused, never slowed down, just kept walking, walking, *walking*, knowing full well that she had no choice but to follow.

*This can't be. He can't be serious about this. He's trying to pull something on me. This is very bad. God, what a horrible place. It reminds me of Mirkwood Forest, all twisted and bent. The stillness is unreal...*

Here the blast's effects had been concentrated. The equivalent of a hundred and fifty-kiloton bomb had exploded almost directly above them, liquefying the skyline in mere seconds, sparing none of the elegant, glass-sheathed towers. They all came down. There was little left. Everything looked wilted, deformed. Squashed into putty by a giant, pressing hand.

*The wasteland.*

What else would you call a place so devoid of life? The light was muted, insubstantial. It had been like that for weeks; occasionally the perpetual overcast would thin a little, but the sun was rarely visible through concealing layers of high, dirty clouds. The grey, impartial light the only source of illumination.

It revealed the devastation. It amplified the silence.

And, everywhere, the smell of the dead.

Kay and her guide crept through the glimmering graveyard. The footing was precipitous; there were yawning depths to be skirted, immense sheets of molten glass and plastic to skip and skitter across. She worried of losing her surly companion and then not being able to find her way out, wandering the ruins until she finally just gave up and crawled into a hole to die. She tried to keep up but he knew the way and, she noticed, he was much stronger and nimbler than he looked.

He was ten yards ahead of her when he stopped and rapped on a panel directly beneath his feet.

Three quick—two slow—three quick

She joined him, caught her breath as they waited.

"What now?"

"Be quiet!" The answering knock came two or three minutes later, a single, subterranean *thump*. He looked at her. "Well, babe, this is as far as I go." The sneer was back. Her eyes flicked down to the door. "What are you waiting for? Go on...open it." Still she didn't move. "Go on, *babe*. Or maybe you ain't as tough as you let on."

*You could be right*, she admitted. But only to herself.

For Sebastian.

She reached down, gripped the improvised rope handle and pulled. The door was heavy and it took two attempts to drag it open. And then she had to jump back because she misjudged its momentum and nearly got flattened. He just stood there, laughing. He told her she was "funnier than Mr. Bean".

A crude ladder led down into a dirt-walled cavity, the floor of which was not visible. She took a deep breath and stepped on to the ladder, started down, counting the rungs as she went. *Two. Three. Five...*

"Tell 'em Kenny sent you," he called to her as he shut the door, depriving her of what little light she'd had.

She descended slowly, lingering a moment on each successive rung before reluctantly moving on. Her eyes weren't adjusting to the stifling black; she could see nothing, not even the ladder itself. What happened when it ran out?

Ten steps later, she had her answer.

It was like the ground came rushing up to meet her, her questing foot colliding with something indisputably solid and unyielding. Her relief was just as palpable. Followed immediately thereafter by terror, the most intense jolt of fear she had ever experienced. Deep-rooted and dating back to childhood.

She'd always been scared of the dark.

Kay followed along the wall until she found an opening to a tunnel. It wasn't very wide and she kept stumbling on the uneven floor. Somewhere down there was something alive—it moaned and muttered intermittently, strange syllables that didn't sound human.

*Nothing to be afraid of. Time to get on with the job, girl.* But she got turned around somehow, tripped and went face first into the wall. She dabbed gingerly at her nose. She'd furled a little flap of skin on the tip, *just a scratch really, nothing a little makeup won't cover, ha, ha!*

*Shit! Gotta take it slow and try to remember how to get out of here again.* Groping her way along, she became aware that the grumbling was getting louder; it now approximated some kind of language but she still couldn't make out any words.

The tunnel took a sudden turn and she was among them.

A few candles provided adequate illumination but it was her nose that supplied the first convincing evidence as to the identity of the inhabitants of the grotto:

Scabs.

*That rotten bastard led me into a den of Scabs.*

Of all the post-apocalyptic horror stories, the Scabs had acquired the special distinction of being the single most repugnant living examples of the perversity of nuclear war.

Their ranks were composed of those survivors who were closest to ground zero. Flying glass and debris should have eviscerated them, the intense heat and radiation should have fried them outright...somehow, the Scabs had survived.

They were doomed to short life spans, of course, their bodies wracked with pain, constantly malfunctioning, betraying them with cruel relentlessness.

Some were blind, many were missing limbs, most were undoubtedly mad.

All bore the hideous stigmata from which their nickname was derived: the *keloids*, layered scar tissue that swelled their faces and puckered their flesh.

Almost immediately they came to be hated, shunned as living manifestations of a war that had killed so many mothers and fathers and sisters and brothers. The common people might be forgiven for their abominable behavior but the Scabs fared no better with medical staffs when they sought help. Most doctors considered them terminal cases and refused to treat them, often denying them even a modicum of kindness and civility: a sip of bottled water, a smile, a reassuring word.

The Scabs quickly learned that there was no place for them in the New Society currently under construction. They retreated to those regions of the city deemed unfit for habitation by the others. How they survived, no one was certain. It was presumed that like everybody else they looted abandoned stores and that led to talk of cleaning them out once and for all, seizing all the goods they had accumulated and distributing it among those who could put the stuff to better use.

Nothing had come of the idea…not yet anyway. Better, maybe, to let them rot away.

That's what Kay's nose had detected: the rot. Untended, infected tissue falling away from faces and hands and feet, leaving mere remnants of people, a form of living death.

She had to get out of there, leave, *right now*. She started to turn around and had just given the order to her feet, *girls, this is a red alert, I need warp speed in two seconds or we're all dead*, when—

"You'll never make it," the scab hissed as he pushed himself up from one of the low benches that lined the walls. The others still seated stared at her, her appearance remarked upon by the same gruff utterances she'd heard earlier.

"I-I'm sorry. I didn't know—"

A hand rose painstakingly. "Doesn't matter. What do you want?"

"I want to leave. I'll go and—"

"You go and you *die*." She choked on her heart. "You stay and you might live. *Might*."

"What do you want me to do?"

"What have you got for us?" She twisted out of the backpack, held it out to him by the straps. "Empty it. On here." He tapped a desk that had once seated a small child. Kay shuffled over to where he stood, blanching at the smell his body gave off, avoiding looking at him. She opened the pack, removed some oranges, an apple and a small head of lettuce. "That's all? Most of us..." Something in his voice drew her eyes to his face. He had no lips. His yellow-white teeth were still surprisingly intact, prominent against his blackened gums. When he spoke, his teeth remained locked together, his jaw rigid, words torturously formed. "Most of us have trouble with solid food."

"I...brought this." She pulled out the real prize: almost a

quart of milk. Some in the chamber sucked in their breath, began to rise from their seats. The authoritative scab waved them back. They subsided, grumbling ominously.

"That's good. That's very good." A pocked hand stroked the jar. "What do you want from us?"

"Pills," she blurted. "Antibiotics. My husband...he's dying, his immune system's crashing and he's dying. I need," she took a deep breath, "*he* needs antibiotics. Whatever you have."

"Who told you about us?"

"Kenny. He said his name was Kenny."

The Scab nodded. "I think we might have what you're looking for." She forced herself to look at him, smiled gratefully. "And these items should cover the cost."

"Thank you, I—"

"Pack this up and put it over there." Kay did as she was told. When she returned the desktop had been raised and he was rummaging within. He handed her several large vials. "Penicillin." He proffered another batch. "Codeine. Demerol." Some of the others made sounds of complaint but he ignored them. Finally he closed the lid, watched as Kay stuffed the precious vials into her pockets.

She was elated. She had conquered her fears, shown great courage in the face of adversity and accomplished what she came to do. But now she desperately wanted to leave this place. Despite the charity the creature had shown her, she still didn't feel safe among his kind. She was alone, an *outsider*, and no one, besides Kenny, knew where she was. Not a good strategy. She started backing toward the passage.

"I—I want to thank you for—"

"No." The abrupt coldness of the single syllable made her shiver. "You owe."

"But I paid you for the pills!"

"For the pills, yes, for your life, *no*."

She felt heavy all over. "I have nothing left to trade."

The desktop rose again. The scab reached in and withdrew a polished scalpel, its silver cast reflecting the feeble light of a nearby candle onto the walls and ceiling.

"Yes, you do…"

The others moved up behind her, clutching at her with swollen, misshapen hands, their doughy faces looming before her, pressing in on her. She tried to scream but couldn't find her breath. She was blacking out, fading away, leaving the scene of the crime.

"Such a beautiful woman," the Scab crooned. "So smooth...so untouched."

He was close, very close, she could see his eyes and they were green and she had always liked green eyes, *Sebastian has green eyes, greenish-blue and—oh my God, he's cutting me...*

And then a tottering, faltering flight.

She managed to rip a sleeve off her shirt and knot it around her forearm, directly above the wound. That stopped most of the bleeding.

It was funny, but her arm didn't hurt. Not even a little bit. It was like it was someone else's arm. She thought the lack of pain was suspicious. *Abnormal.* Like those red trees over there...

Kay came to the abrupt realization that for the past— well, she couldn't say *how* long, exactly—she had been sleep-walking, blundering down desolate avenues in a fugue state, completely oblivious to her surroundings. It was a wonder she hadn't fallen into an open elevator shaft. She decided to pull up a chunk of rubble, make herself comfortable until the spell passed.

Some of it was coming back now. She remembered the scalpel and how just *touching* her with the blade had broken the skin and how it felt when it slid into her flesh, biting quick and hard...but her brain obstinately refused to allow her to re-experience the pain that must have accompanied the sensation.

What Kay wished she could forget, what she wished could be excised from her mind forever was their excitement as blood bubbled from the wound, the way they had fought each other and when one gained predominance—

—how it had positioned its mouth over the slit, slurping and lapping at the blood, gulping audibly, grunting in obscene satisfaction.

Until another pushed it aside and took its turn.

She wasn't sure how long it had gone on; at some point the flow subsided. As she swooned she could hear latecomers snarling in disappointment.

Had they released her or had she broken away from

them, fought her way free and bolted down the tunnel to the ladder?

It didn't matter.

She was alive and she'd gotten what she came for. Patting her pockets.

*Little boxes of miracles...*

She sure hoped they lived up to their billing.

Because after what she'd just been through she *needed* a sign, some indication that there was still a god up there, someone who forgave our trespasses and listened to the simple prayers of a woman living in the valley of the shadow of death.

## Notes on the Stories
### by Cliff Burns

*"Apocalypse Beach"*  Originally intended for a short story collection centered around nuclear war I put together back in the mid-1980s. I believe I wrote "Apocalypse Beach" not long after returning from a whirlwind road trip to Los Angeles with my buddy Jim. I used to like leading off public readings with this one, love the way it delivers a "short, sharp shock". It quickly set the mood and let folks know they were in for an unusual evening of entertainment.

*"Invisible Boy"*  Destined to be one of my signature short stories, one that definitely comes from the heart. There were many times during my childhood when I either felt invisible or wished I had the ability to disappear, fade away. "Invisible Boy" has been anthologized a couple of times and a number of readers have written to me about how it's affected them and

evoked powerful emotions and memories. It remains a special, special tale.

*"Walt Disney in Hell: A Trilogy"* The kind, genteel Timothy Findley *loved* this story. I think it was the one he liked best (which only goes to show what sort of twisted mind lurked beneath that sweet, affable exterior). Another one I enjoyed reading at public events. Made the punters sit up in their seats and pay attention, I'll tell you that. Disney represents everything that is crass, commercial and vulgar about America. *Corporate* entertainment...what a revolting notion.

*"Carl"* Entirely invented, fictional...except I've encountered female predators and they can be every bit as persistent and aggressive as their male counterparts. The title character is a chronic victim, a passive observer when it comes to his own life...until he can no longer allow others to use him for their own selfish purposes. I like the narrator's voice—you get the impression they're really enjoying recounting Carl's sad story, no matter how much they might pretend otherwise.

*"The Cattletruck"* This one has always resonated with readers, a brief episode from a possible future, an encounter with lasting consequences for all involved. The original version had a more overtly Christian (and less effective) last line. This slightly "remastered" take is far better, in every respect. Another tale from my unrealized nuclear war collection, an idea I conceived on a 2½ day train trip to Ottawa (courtesy a timely Canada Council grant). The story coming together as the country revealed itself through narrow, streaked windows and the miles rolled by beneath those steel wheels.

*"The Strange Music"* A story that holds a special place in my heart. It *poured* out in a couple of drafts, arriving (almost) fully formed. It manages to pack a lot into a few pages, a whole family history alluded to but left unexplored. The reader thrust into a drama already in progress (or very near the end), the tension palpable, an explosion imminent. There's an authenticity present throughout, a sense that we're eavesdropping on a private moment. *Love* this tale, the vast depths it hints at.

*"The End"* The quietest piece in the collection, a welcome respite after the previous stories. A three-hander, heavy on dialogue and character, the plot nowhere in sight. I have no doubt if they announced the end of the world was, officially, noon tomorrow, in the morning there would still be a certain percentage of people who would show up for work like it was just another day. Some derive their sanity from ordered, well-delineated lives, complete with regular routines and rote duties. What can I say? It takes all kinds...

*"Snow Angels"* A last minute addition to the collection but I honestly think it holds up well. Emotionally much warmer than the story it replaces ("The Murder of John Lennon: A Collage") and, again, there's a past history that's only alluded to, never explored. This couple is suffering horribly...and who can blame them for seeking solace beyond the pall of normal existence?

*"Sex\*Tet: A Horrific Medley of Old Favorites"* Prose poems with an intent to injure. Much of this collection was written during a period of time when "splatter" or "extreme" horror

was in vogue. This was my reaction to those extended orgies of violence and male rape fantasies. Snuff fiction. I opted to make the grotesque as up close, personal and *unpleasant* as I could. Squirm-inducing...but keep in mind these pieces should also be read in terms of *parody*. Hyperbolic, shocking...with a streak of black, *black* humor running throughout.

*"Teenage Wasteland"* Definitely *not* a true story...though I've run into a few "Lyles" in my time and it's almost always entertaining. I like the banter between the characters—Jamie seems very real to me. Dunno if anyone out there has ever tried Lyle's recipe for growing superior pot but if you *have*, please write and inform us of the results of your experiment. That is, if you can still hold a pen...

*"Public Enemy"* Inspired by the quiet ones, the neighbor you'd never suspect, the loner who always bought cigarettes and a newspaper, paying with exact change. The agents of terror, revolution and rebellion aren't always bomb-throwers and hate-spewers. The most resourceful, *dangerous* fanatics

are virtually undetectable, living right alongside us, making their secret plans.

*"Dry"* A tale right out of a volume by one of my early influences: Richard Matheson, Charles Beaumont or even Ray Bradbury (the first SF book I can remember reading was his collection *The Golden Apples of the Sun*). Intriguing premise, sympathetic characters and a nice twist at the end. *Your next stop, the Twilight Zone.* Not artistically adventurous or earth-shattering, perhaps, but I'll bet there are a good number of farmers out there who will relate to this tale, the heart-rending decision Hal McCarthy is confronted with.

*"Old Friends"* Is our old pal Mr. D the Devil or a sales representative of the spooky guy with the scythe? *Or* is he merely that little voice advising us to ignore common sense, do something crazy, prove we're still alive? There are good and bad angels in our nature and *most* of the time the guys in white hats win out and we live to see another day. But...there are always exceptions to that rule.

*"Live! From Planet Earth!"* Some comedy to leaven the prevailing grimness. All right, so it's black comedy. All right, so it's a black comedy about the annihilation of the human race. All right, so it's a black comedy about the annihilation of the human race that concludes with a station break. It's still bloody amusing, don't you think?

*"Man Disassembling"* Another gorgeous little vignette. Short, definitely not sweet. *Fantastic* last line. A monologue on isolation, automation, what it means to be human. Equal parts Phil Dick and Sam Beckett—caught with my influences hanging out and flapping in the breeze (yet again).

*"Arrival"* I'm *not* a fan of H.P. Lovecraft's writing. I find it turgid, tuneless and not infrequently cringeworthy. But I'm fascinated by his cosmology, the notion of ancient beings biding their time, itching to gain a toehold in our universe and wreak havoc. By the time I'd written this story I'd already received over five hundred rejection letters—do you think the frustration is starting to show?

*"Final Showing"* As I've stated elsewhere, I believe there are hierarchies, even in Hell. "Final Showing" is one of my most flat out moralistic stories, a villain receiving his proper comeuppance. Rough justice...but what do you expect in Hell?

*"Monologue"* My father was Irish and could swear like a world champion. Long strings of expletives erupting from his mouth with an ease and fluency that astonished those within earshot. He possessed admirable diction, venom and peerless rhythm. I drew on his memory when devising the narrator's inner dialogue. There's lots of dad's frustrated rage and unbridled racism in this tale. I used to close my readings with this one, which usually led to pin-drop silences that went on and on...

*"The Hibakusha"* If memory serves me correctly, this tale came courtesy a dream. In the dream I never actually saw who was there, in the dark with me, but I clearly *heard* them, snuffling and grunting, and I knew, somehow, that these creatures were hideous in appearance, with claws and pincers of flesh for hands. This is the scariest story I've ever written, a

plausible scenario told with almost documentary-like realism. One that continues to haunt me thirty years after its conception.

CLIFF BURNS is the author of a number of previous novels and short story collections, including *So Dark the Night*, *The Last Hunt* and *Exceptions and Deceptions*. His work has been featured in magazines and anthologies around the world and adapted for the radio and stage. He lives in western Canada with his wife, Sherron.